White Book / Pavel Kohout

White Book

Adam Juráček, Professor of Drawing

and Physical Education at

the Pedagogical Institute in K.,

vs.

Sir Isaac Newton, Professor of Physics

at the University of Cambridge,

Reconstructed from Contemporary

Records and Supplemented by Most

Interesting Documents by

Pavel Kohout

George Braziller　　　　／　　　　New York

For Pierrot

Translated by Alex Page

Library of Congress Cataloging in Publication Data
Kohout, Pavel.
  White book.

  Translation of Weissbuch.
  I. Title.
PZ3.K8199Wh3 [PG5038.K64] 891.8'6'35 76–55846
ISBN 0–8076–0861–0

First Printing
Printed in the United States of America

Contents

Prologue

Epilogue

Prologue

RECONSTRUCTION 1

(According to contemporary records)

When
in the morning of March 4, 19--,
in the resort town of K. at 1 Park Street,
Mrs. Josefa Juráčková, born Hopnerová, widow of a train conductor,
rose at the usual hour and performed a series of long-familiar tasks, resulting in a substantial breakfast for
her only son Adam Juráček, Professor of Drawing and Physical Education at the Pedagogical Institute of K., and then
carried the tray, teapot sparkling, eggs gleaming white, to the door of her son's room to indicate with a knock that the food was ready and placed in the doorway, she listened in vain for the agreed-upon response, namely, a
low whistle, whereupon she took courage in maternal solicitude to disregard the commandment he had expressly laid upon her three months ago, turned the handle, opened the door, stepped with the tray intact over the threshold into the living quarters of her son and instantly emitted a cry

of horror, clapped her hands to her mouth so that the tray, abruptly deprived of all support, yielded to the

law of gravity and dropped its entire cargo to the floor, all of which was occasioned by the fact that the aforementioned son of Josefa Juráčková, Professor of Drawing and Physical Education at the Pedagogical Institute of K., in harsh conflict with said law,

stood on the ceiling,

his body projecting down, head foremost, parallel to the chromeplated rod of the light fixture, and the expression on his face that floated between the two white globes reflected a certain embarrassment, the mother of the professor released a mere

sigh when a voice came from above:

"Mama, don't be afraid, don't worry, I'll explain everything . . ."

whereupon Josefa Juráčková began to crisscross the not very spacious room, her arms outstretched, uttering strange sounds like

"eps, eps . . ."

until he understood and shouted to her:

"don't look for steps, I'm o.k., Mama, hold on a minute, Mama . . ."

as she passed for the third time under the lamp he managed to catch her hand but contrary to expectation this didn't yank him to the ground, instead he successfully slowed his mother's careening and brought it to a stop without altering his position, which she became aware of despite her confusion so that she broke into loud crying, and now it was his turn to be frightened.

"For God's sake, please, Mama, don't, look, Mama, I'll be right with you . . ."

and with these words he detached himself from the ceiling and sank as gracefully to the floor as when he showed his students at the school swimming pool how to dive, but not even then was she calmed as she sat on the chair which he

4

had thoughtfully drawn close and as she glanced with moist eyes upon the debris of china and egg yolk, so he spoke to her more urgently:

"Mama, Mama dear, listen to me, don't cry, damn it, listen, stop your bawling . . ."

it was not his way to raise his voice, certainly not when talking to his mother, whom he admired for all she had endured since the day they had had to give up the company apartment above the Lower Station in K. owing to the one and only lapse of the blessed husband and father, the train conductor, an apartment from the windows of which one enjoyed a view of a

small platform and siding, calling to mind a toy train. He shouted at her most unwillingly, but saw at the moment no other way, surprisingly she stopped crying, and when he took her face in his hands and turned it towards him, he had her take hold of herself so that he could speak in the hope of being heard, he said to her in all probability, almost certainty, as it becomes evident from documents, accounts of witnesses, and a detailed examination of his life, his thinking, and his habits, he said quickly something like this in somewhat this way:

"Mama, dear silly Mama, though there's a chance I might be late for class, and I'm supposed to impart them the secret of drawing perspective, never mind, I'm going to stay here with you until I have explained everything to you, the heart of what you saw and upset you so much, then you'll understand, Mama dear, that it's just as obvious as perspective and not more dangerous than a handstand, and that you are eventually going to be tickled pink by it, everyone, Mama, has his fantasies and desires, some may at first seem ridiculous, foolish, and therefore you don't dare mention them, human life is an opportunity nature offers to each of her most advanced organisms so that the individual may fulfil himself by bringing about the longed-for aim, and, at best, improve with his achievement the living conditions of his entire species. Such are Euclid, Archimedes, Galileo and

Newton," Adam Juráček continued in growing excitement,

"not to mention Einstein, whose sweet aroma still lingers in our atmosphere, glowing examples all of them, you know, dear Mama, how I was always shy and timid, how rarely you hid your misgivings, although you put before me less exalted models than those I mentioned, namely, Bohuslav Voráček, once my schoolmate, today the director of my school, the problem being, Mama, that despite my reticence and shyness —you never had an idea—my dreams were always more ambitious than Voráček's, I don't want to harp on that, too much bitterness there, except for the last one, the dream that became real before your eyes. As professor in my discipline I always clashed with a basic law in physics, formulated so concisely and firmly especially in the high jump which I teach to all grades, there it seemed to me painfully humbling to have to cope with the limitation which gravity imposes upon the human body and from the moment my student Václav Klokoč, tops in everything else, positively failed to clear the bar at 100 centimeters, this conflict of mine became torture. One thing has become

clear to me," the professor continued, stroking his mother's hair,

"that he made it possible for me to take the right path at the very outset, namely that a law of physics cannot be revoked by physical force, but by a force, Mama, which you least suspected me to possess, the force of will. So I concentrated with all I had upon attaining that will power, which explains the oriental and Sokol* tunes you heard in my room, explains the many restrictions which I saddled myself with, and alas you too, for instance, the plastic Christmas

*Sokol: the oldest Czech physical fitness organization, founded in 1862, and playing an important part in the national revival movement and in the political life of Bohemia. Sokol tunes accompanied all, especially athletic, events.

tree I left you with at Christmas, it explains the many tests to which I voluntarily submitted myself and which caused you anxiety about my physical and mental well-being. But, Mama, never did I feel better than in the days I denied myself the pleasures I had earlier enjoyed. As so often in the history of the world, the actual key to success came to me via a humdrum incident when in my drawing class the worst dummy among my juniors, Kreperát, set fire to the wastepaper basket in the corner of the classroom with a very ordinary magnifying glass, in that second before the fire department arrived it came to me how sunlight gives off its energy only when its scattered rays form a light-cone, similarly the will can be turned into a mechanical force only when the scattered thoughts are formed into one mighty

concentrate, that was the moment," said the professor enthusiastically,

"when I began, dear Mama, to give you cause for the deepest concern as well as, I feared, the anger of another person very dear to me, Kateřina Horová, when I begged her for a three-month break in our relationship just in order to insure its later happy conclusion. I lied to you and to her, Mama, when I said I was preparing myself for another degree in Physical Education, whereas in reality I focused my inner self upon one single idea, I did this everywhere, in the street, in the stadium, when I lectured, and of course primarily in this room. I learned how to respond to a greeting mechanically, make my replies mere reflexes, eat automatically, nothing existed for me, Mama, apart from one single aim, an aim twelve feet high, the exact distance from floor to ceiling, I stared at it, I fixed on it all night, yes, Mama, I confess that in the last few weeks I slept very little, but please don't be angry, it had to be. Archimedes was stabbed on account of his circles and Galileo tortured for his calculations, look how the danger I was in was many times smaller, merely a matter of giving myself wholly to my own thoughts, to de-individualize myself, to lose my specific gravity, and above all, with the aid of the imagination, acquire a new angle of vision of all the objects in the room in order not to lose my balance at the critical moment. I don't deny it was grinding work, Mama, every bit of it, but worthy of its cause, far from a trivial cause, to free mankind from its archaic bonds, because airplanes and rockets merely obscured the great aim, for as soon as the thrust of the motors ceased, man dropped back to earth like a rock, I don't want to recall my father, the train conductor, but even his dim memory supported me, week after week I stretched myself toward the ceiling, fixed my eyes upon the tiniest flaw left by the brush of the painter. Twice indeed I had the sensation of weighing no more than an ounce, twice the ceiling rippled like the surface of a pond when it's hit by the air mass preceding a diver, but twice it was that very ounce by which I outweighed my thought. Surely I would have fallen into

deep despair," said Adam Juráček, clasping his mother's hands in his,

"but not even despair could penetrate the bulwark of my concentration. Now I know at this moment as my thinking returns to normal that just at that time my ability to concentrate grew in geometric progression, it was like a free fall, Mama, but like a fall upwards, and at the end of it came the moment whose unexpected witness you became, since only this morning without a sign or premonition the ceiling approached, at first imperceptibly, then faster and faster until it suddenly but gently tipped and my field of vision was of the floor, my couch, the table, and the chairs, it happened so smoothly and so utterly naturally, Mama, as when I had looked down from the cupboard in order to accustom myself to it, only infinitely more comfortable and less dangerous. The ceiling supported me quite as securely as the floor had done before, I succeeded in turn in sitting, in kneeling and finally in standing up, and that's when you entered, and that jarred my composure, Mama. In my exercises I hadn't counted on such a contingency, I felt as though you'd fall on top of me before I realized that the force of gravity of which I had rid myself continued to safeguard you, nevertheless, Mama, it is

fantastic," Professor Adam Juráček laughed triumphantly, stood up and clapped his hands with unconcealed delight,

"that in that moment, you see, when my surprise wiped out all other thoughts, I remained up there, don't you see, dear Mama, what that means, that my feeling of self-detachment *independent of* my present state of mind has begun to operate, that it has ceased to be a feeling and has become a *faculty,* just as a jumble of foreign words suddenly condenses into knowledge of that language, or as attempts at drawing metamorphose into art, beginning with this moment I can always achieve the same result, whenever I wake in me the need for self-detachment and without having to go through my ascetic regimen, from now on,"

declared Professor Adam Juráček solemnly, rising, his hands slightly upraised, toward the ceiling of his room,

"man is physically free, for a law once broken ceases to be law."

He did not finish his explanation because Mrs. Josefa Juráčková, born Hopnerová, widow of the train conductor, and his mother, again broke into tears, but when he lowered himself lightning-quick to her chair in order to renew his consolations, he discovered that her eyes showed no sign of despair.

"O son, son of mine," the mother cried, "am I proud of you!"

STATEMENT

by Vilibald Bláha, Professor of Physics at the Pedagogical Institute of K., given on March 5, 19--, at 10:45 A.M.

(With notations by Examiner, Police Sgt. Vilém Hrad)

I address myself to the events that transpired yesterday afternoon, March 4, 19--, in the faculty room of the Pedagogical Institute of K.

As we do every Thursday, we met at 2:00 P.M. in the faculty room of the Pedagogical Institute of K. in order to go over our work so far and to agree on a syllabus for the coming week.

At the outset of the meeting the Director of the Pedagogical Institute of K., Comrade B. Voráček, found it necessary to reprimand a member of the faculty, namely, A. Juráček, Professor of Drawing and Physical Education. Professor Juráček had failed to meet his drawing class which he was supposed to have held at 8:00 A.M. The students promptly exploited his absence by leaving for home. An unidentified student spread the rumor that measles had broken out. Consequently the schedules of a number of professors were disrupted, mine among them, since I had planned to give that very class at 11:20 A.M. a quiz on the material covered in physics. I brought this up during the ensuing discussion and requested Professor Juráček to make up my loss by giving me one of his classes in drawing or physical education in fair exchange.

Professor Juráček, who had acted in a perfectly normal manner so far and whom I had taken to be a quiet, modest type of man, made the most astonishing comment that the loss of an hour's class in physics could have done the students no harm.

Yes, he displayed a certain nervousness. I assume that was owing to his reprimand.

Of course I countered with the argument that we are living in an age of a scientific-technological revolution. I pointed out that leading politicians have emphasized time and again the importance of the natural sciences, a fact plainly evident in the new curricula and the expanded class hours assigned to mathematics, chemistry, and physics.

No, I do not in any way mean to question the importance of physical education. I am fully aware that it toughens enormously the defensive capability of our country. That is why at that point I didn't want to tangle with Professor Juráček any further.

But he went right on to explain that a scientific-technological revolution in particular demanded of teachers not to hang on to outdated dogmas but rather to keep making sure that the natural laws they taught remained valid. At this point I permitted myself the observation that these laws were discovered by reputable scientists and not by monkey drillmasters.

Yes, I grant Professor Juráček had reason to feel offended. In my defense I can only state that at that moment I thought he was plain drunk.

Yes, I agree it was an unfounded charge because it was known to me that my colleague Juráček is in tip-top physical condition, neither smokes nor drinks, and leads an exemplary private life.

Yes, it is true, I am divorced, I smoke and occasionally I take a little wine.

No, absolutely not. I declare categorically that I have never abused the privileges of the physics lab for purposes of sexual intercourse. My proof is that I am 58.

(Subject begs for permission to make an uninterrupted statement as the questions confuse him and undermine his powers of concentration. He is reminded that the ability to respond to questions quickly belongs to the basic equipment of a high school instructor.)

Professor Juráček reacted to my inappropriate remark in a manner that seemed even more inappropriate.

(Subject is cautioned to deal with the matter at hand and refrain from personal judgments.)

Professor Juráček went on to say that distinguished pioneers deserved at least this much, that their successors would not turn science into a trade. I am not going to conceal the displeasure evoked by this, not only in me but in the other faculty members who felt called upon to support me and to insist on an explanation.

Their names? Mrs. Sováková, Professor of Mathematics and Descriptive Geometry, and our colleague Krbálek, Professor of Chemistry.

(Make this info part of the respective dossiers of the above-named for possible later scrutiny.)

Professor Juráček declared to our amazement that he had in mind the law concerning earth's gravity. We all laughed, I admit. At that moment we were to a man convinced that our colleague Juráček had been drinking, for which, as I earlier stated, there was no solid evidence. But I wish to point out that even Comrade Director Voráček, who had been Juráček's schoolmate and therefore knew him better than anyone, asked whether he hadn't in mind the gravitational attraction of the eternal feminine.

(Look into the circumstances surrounding Comrade Voráček's appointment to the directorship of the Pedagogical Institute of K.)

Professor Adam Juráček informed us that he was thinking of the law of gravity as propounded by the immortal Sir Isaac Newton.

And who is he—is that your question? I wish to state that the immortal Sir Isaac Newton was a professor at Cambridge.

Very well, I shall amplify: Cambridge is in England.

No, I could not possibly have known said individual personally since he was born in 1643. What immortalized him was that very law of gravity expounded in his work of 1687, the *Philosophiae Naturalis Principia Mathematica*. It is my considered view that we are talking of the greatest mind of the second millenium. His mortal remains were interred in Westminster Abbey. In 1937 I had saved enough money from my teaching assistantship to go and pay him my respects in person.

(At this point subject began to cry, and he shrieked the last sentence over again. A doctor had to be summoned who made him take a tranquillizer so that by 1:15 P.M. the examination could resume.)

Now it became clear that Professor Juráček had really meant it. It was me upon whom devolved the duty of presenting a reasoned case in opposition—a duty by virtue of my academic oath, of the confidence reposed in me by my colleagues, and above all by virtue of the shining memory of the immortal Sir Isaac Newton.

(Subject began to cry again. A psychologist was called in who recommended that subject be left alone in the room and that he make his statement on a tape recorder. The following is a transcript of the tape.)

"What am I to say? Good gracious God, what more can I say? Elizabeta, have I lost you for nothing?"

(Subsequent investigation reveals that the reference is to subject's former wife. She allegedly left him owing to an habitual neglect of his marital duties and found refuge with her parents in Bardějov.)

"This muscle man and shmeer artist . . . how can I erase this tape? Gentlemen, my apologies, I am nervous. But my colleague Juráček erased with one sentence a law that holds the universe together, yes, I said and mean the universe, gentlemen, even this moron Havelka, a junior, can tell you that gravitation, from Latin *gravis,* heavy, force, weight, applying to the force of attraction generally, that is, the mutual gravitational pull of two masses m_1 and m_2 is according to Newton's law of gravity, listen to me, Elizabeta, is in a direct ratio to the product of two masses and the inverse ratio to the square of their distance from each other. Even a Havelka can give you, without having to think, this miracle of a formula, $F = k \frac{m_1 \times m_2}{r^2}$, where F is the force which two masses at the distance r exert on each other. Yes, there you have it, that's the gravitational constant, Elizabeta, of which you said, 'either it or me . . .' "

(The tape registers sobbing.)

"And I gave it priority because I knew . . . knew? Believed, yes, had faith, still have faith . . ."

(Subject strikes table, a pause, he continues in a calmer tone as though he had taken hold of himself.)

"Gravitation is a force by means of which the earth affects the objects on its surface. That much, my dear colleague Juráček, you have certainly learned, and you're its living witness, gravitation being that force that even holds the planets in their elliptical orbits, holds the solar system together, the entire cosmos. What don't you like, my esteemed colleague, what rubs you the wrong way, you, a Professor of Physical Education and Drawing, what displeases you about the law of gravity promulgated by the immortal Sir Isaac Newton? He looked straight at me, gentlemen, such eyes I saw only once before in my life . . . when you asked me, Elizabeta, 'it or me?' "

(Pause.)

"And then he said, literally said: 'A law once broken ceases to be law.' I yelled at him, I admit I yelled, and I don't give a damn."

(Table is struck, noises indicating attempts to reverse the tape, some unintelligible phrases, then in a low voice.)

". . . or else I know nothing, can't make heads or tails of anything. I said to him: 'Can you perhaps imagine, dear colleague, that as of today a stone falls *up?*' And he said, 'No, dear colleague,' he said, 'I can't, not a stone, but I believe a rational being can succeed. . . .' Gentlemen, at that moment I read in the eyes of the assembled faculty exactly my own thoughts. 'You are crazy, Juráček,' I yelled, 'you've lost your mind,' Comrade Director, this man must instantly be put in the hands of a psychiatrist, either he goes or I . . . either me or gravity . . . Elizabeta, I loved you . . . either me or Juráček, Comrade Director, for we have responsibilities to Havelka and all the other growing students, what are they going to think of us?"

(The tape registers steps, subject is evidently pacing the room, his voice rises and falls, becomes at times unintelligible.)

"Two bodies attract each other, Comrade Director, with a force, Professor Juráček, in direct ratio to their masses, Elizabeta, and inverse ratio to the square of their distance, which we designate by r. And it makes no difference whatever, gentlemen, if you are that body or the globe, that's the law, older than the Bible, which not even the immortal Sir Isaac Newton . . . and I personally paid him my respects . . . his mortal remains are interred in Westminster Abbey,

(Subject is shouting.)

and I challenge you to verify it . . . not even the great Newton made it up, he merely discovered it and offered proof, and you, Juráček, you owe it to this law that your students when they do their high jump don't fly off into outer space but fall back to earth so they can get to my physics class where a sounder instruction awaits them . . ."

(A pause, heavy breathing.)

"And he said: 'What is it actually you want, dear colleague, you want proof?' 'Yes, proof, proof, proof, proof, proof!' "

(A long pause.)

"And he stared at the ceiling . . . well . . . and I still had no idea . . . and then . . ."

(A long pause, then a scream.)

"Gentlemen, what have I learned in my whole life? Why

oh why, Elizabeta, did I leave you for that shithead New-ton?"

(Subject proceeded to demolish the furniture in the inter-rogation room. At 2:10 P.M. he was taken to the psychiatric section of the local clinic in K. This document necessarily breaks off without subject's signature. Transmitted to Com-rade Nohýnek for evaluation.)

RECONSTRUCTION 2

(According to contemporary records)

When he saw

looking down that Mrs. Sováková, Professor of Mathe-matics and Descriptive Geometry, had fainted while the other members of the faculty were absolutely frozen, he quickly lowered himself in order to render her assistance. He removed from his breast pocket a white handkerchief which he had kept in readiness for three months and, without hesi-tation, wetted it although the

tears of Kateřina Horová clung to it, it brought her to mind and for a second he experienced the love that

cancelled everything else, but the voice of the elderly lady brought him back to the present, she opened her eyes, smiled at him as though from a distance:

"You know, Adam," she said, hesitating, "it suddenly seemed you were walking on the ceiling,"

words of which he was going to be reminded, and could he have had a notion what they meant and under what circumstances they would be repeated, he would have

acted otherwise, but for the time being it was enough for him to return to his chair and, without the least tremor, read over the syllabus for the coming week. It could be confidently claimed that every single member of the faculty, not excluding Director Voráček, shared the same feeling, namely, that each had touched

the bare ends of a charged wire, and that they ought to have gone home with a funny taste in their mouths and sick at heart at the thought that they had passed the peak of their productive powers and were plummeting in a free fall into the arms of arteriosclerosis, but no one would have mentioned a

syllable of this to anyone else. Adam Juráček was equally shaken, his mother's reaction that morning, although accompanied by the clatter of glass, had found relief in tears of pride, and he had forgotten that love for a son swells in the bosom of a mother whether he is a forger or even a mass murderer, for mothers do not grasp the quality of their sons' deeds, merely their magnitude, so that at night they can whisper into the darkness with a thrill,

"O God, what a thing to have nurtured beneath my heart...."

But now he displayed his talent to people who weren't prepared for it, either professionally or humanly, nor had that been his intention in the first place. When in the morning he had stretched himself on his back so astonishingly solid upon the ceiling of his room, above him, like being sentenced to the Damoclean swords of cupboard, bookcase, couch, table, and chairs, himself protected by the lampshade, he felt that even the way of the Cross could lead to a happy

end. He hadn't had an easy childhood. After the albeit sole lapse of his father, the train conductor, he and his mother had had to leave the company apartment above the Lower Station, at the windows of which apartment he had spent every free minute, loving above all the view of the small

platform and siding that reminded one of a toy train, and when he was six he knew the departure and arrival times of the trains perfectly, he knew the signals and gestures of the railworkers, before going to sleep he checked the positions of the warning signals, and in his dream he took over the functions of the stationmaster, while in the mornings he calculated how many months and years he had still to wait. When his mother took a job as

housemaid in the Grand Hotel and they moved into the center of the resort, he stopped

speaking, until he was fifteen, he uttered none but the most necessary words, confined himself to minimal communication with mother and teachers, despite maternal tears and slaps he ate no more than his body needed for bare physical survival, his arms and legs were like sticks and he was slightly

hydrocephalous, stuffed with pills, riddled by injections, to no effect. Year after year his teachers considered transferring him to a school for

retarded children, but his mother's begging discouraged them, they were afraid of her because she sank to her knees before them not only at the door of the faculty room but also on the street and in shops, she pursued former Director Kavan on her knees for an entire block while he was showing some foreign visitors around, it brought on his anger and almost his

death, since then no one even dared think about the school for retarded children, anyway they had recommended a transfer to make it easier on themselves, he never had to repeat a grade. Later he was to confide to the only person he was ever completely frank with:

"I don't know why or how, but I have no recollection of those years, as though I had lived through them

unconsciously. . . ." At sixteen he is off to the usual summer camp, because he is taciturn and withdrawn he becomes as always the object of ridicule, they call him 'Adummy,' 'Peanut Squash,' and 'Sleepy,' the last most frequently because they have noticed that it makes the corners of his mouth twitch so crazily, what do they know of the small platform

with siding that reminds one of a toy train. At every meal

they pour tea under his chair and tease him by calling him 'Čuráček,' that is, 'Pisserooney,' in the campfire games he serves as straight-man, he's told to take a step back and topples over a stool, he's supposed to tell a flower by its smell, and they hand him a mammoth dose of sneezing powder, they tell him to look at the moon through the telescope of a coatsleeve, and he nearly drowns in a gush of

water, and just then, amid the cruel laughter, a little child comes tripping, the angelic blond daughter of the camp cook, then only three, she takes him by her hand, looks into his wet eyes and tells him in a nearly adult voice:

"Don't cry, I love you, I am going to marry you, then you can beat them all up. . . ."

This sentence he heard a thousand times over, it stayed with him like a telephone tape recording that recounts theater and movie programs, a sentence that told him, in effect, his life's course, this sentence jerks him out of his helplessness and gives him back his life.

"I'm going to marry you, then you can beat them all up . . ." he whispered to himself until nighttime, then he changed the sequence, and next morning he volunteered for the cross-country race, the camp understood the connection and died

laughing, he was the first at the starting line, stood with his eyes closed.

"Pisserooney is praying, hey, Adummy where's your bride, don't worry, if we have to, we'll haul you back in a wheelbarrow . . ."

They couldn't suspect they were witness to a dress rehearsal of an act he was to bring to fulfilment seventeen years later, that for the first time ever he made his energies converge which were dammed up in him as in a reservoir, the energy of hoarded exertions and words, but also of a

knowledge that no one could have suspected in a notorious under-achiever.

As the starting gun goes off, they laugh at his style:

"He runs like a crippled kangaroo, watch out you don't crack your heels, hold on to those bones . . ."

and the runners disappear into the woods, while the onlookers prepare for their return, forming a lane at the finish line and dropping their pants in order to

water the final stretch for the one they know will be the last, stunned they keep holding their organs as he appears running, exhausted, breathless but as

victor, running past the finish line, ignoring them, running on, holding in his hand . . .

"Shit," yelled the leader of the spout-holding brigade, his chief torturer and classmate Voráček, "and he's even plucked her some heather . . ."

he runs on to the kitchen, next to which a little doll is playing with her doll, both with the same angelic blond hair, the one with the click-clack eyes called Masha, the living doll Kateřina Horová, daughter of the camp cook and of a commercial pilot who without a thought detours daily from his assigned route by a hundred miles in order to

show her off to his passengers and dip his wings to her whereupon the entire camp dies with envy. He runs to her, hands her the heather, and she took his hand and never let it go, since then her father the pilot dipped his wings to both of them, the campers were consumed in rage. That is how he came to know her, and it was of her he thought

today, this very morning, of the fateful explosion of his feelings seventeen years ago, the moment he had done *it*. He hadn't seen her for three months, not her either, he had had to switch

her off three months ago like a light, had had to turn off his feelings the way a whole district of town loses its power when its lines are overloaded, had had to do it, had to recharge himself as he called it, but now that *it* had become reality, he belonged again to

her, she would be his first witness, this very evening in Goat Lane or perhaps sooner, in the shoe store, yes, the first witness, the accident with his mother detracted nothing, his mother he regarded as a part of his own being, Kateřina would be the first, really the first, but then

Professor Bláha uttered those unfortunate words, he was going to give his class a

physics test, and there he stood now with a wet handkerchief in front of Mrs. Sováková, Professor of Mathematics and Descriptive Geometry, surrounded by colleagues who glared at him as though they had just survived an earthquake. He knew that if he were to resume his chair and without tremor read over the syllabus of the coming week, then everything would pass without an

upheaval, the day might have left a sour taste in their mouths and they might have trouble falling asleep, but in the morning they would nevertheless meet in the faculty room, pale, a little uncertain, but deep down

grateful that he was going to leave it at that, that he had blared forth nothing, that he had refrained from comments and asked nothing of them, whereby he would have saved them the need to take a position in face of some

real event, it was one of those seconds in which dice are cast but haven't yet stopped rolling, one can still catch them or cover them with one's hands, replace them in the cup, put the cup in one's pocket, remove one's toga in the middle of the Rubicon and pretend one was going to take a

swim, and explain that our invention, a rig of guillotine and wicker basket, is merely a wood-chopping device, cut into the chain reaction and tell the world that the experiment cannot, alas, be brought to conclusion, since no more than one single atom was to hand, and that one inadvertently

mislaid, the one second in which a single individual determines the future of

the multitudes and Adam Juráček, although until this moment an unknown, ordinary, little Professor of Drawing and Physical Education, heeded like Caesar, Doctor Guillotin, Rutherford, and other geniuses before him a secret command and took upon himself the burden of his mission by saying

"Now perhaps Colleague Bláha is no longer in doubt that gravity can be overcome by will power . . ."

"Comrades," said Director Voráček immediately thereafter, pulling himself together and showing himself worthy of the office entrusted him, "what happened here is so momentous, and momentous doesn't begin to say it, that I declare this meeting top secret, under pain of instant dismissal from all employment on account of untrustworthiness, and I request you to go home as directly as possible and remain there until otherwise notified. This applies most especially to colleague Juráček whom I urge and order to take a taxi home—let someone phone for one—and strictly obey the law of gravity as long as no expert has expressed an opinion as to his discovery. Tomorrow, by order of the Director, there is no school. I will get in touch with Comrade Mareš immediately. I propose you leave right away, quietly, singly. Don't forget for a moment to keep in mind the well-being of your families and your students, then nothing can happen to you that will make you lose your composure and your dignity . . ."

After he had entered his office, Director Voráček opened the window that looked upon the athletic fields of the school, and began to spit through it rhythmically, and, keeping the beat, saying again and again like an incantation:

"Shit, shit, shit."

MINUTES

of a special meeting of the higher administrative officials of town and district K., held on March 5, 19--.

Comrades attending: Kreperát, Hábl, Mareš
Comrades invited: Voráček
Recording secretary: B. Dreiseittelová
Proceedings begin at 2:10 P.M.

Comrade Kreperát wants to know what it's all about. Addressed to the district office, he had received a teletyped message from Comrade Hábl telling him to return immediately as his wife had fallen sick, but at home his son told him she had gone out for a walk and Comrades Hábl and Mareš were expecting him.

Comrade Hábl would like to point out at the outset that he thought it best if Comrade Kreperát, he, and Comrade Mareš constituted themselves into a three-man board in order to confer among themselves. He finds we ought to agree upon some kind of line, a common point-of-view, which we can adhere to when having to face up to both higher and lower echelons, in order not to put our foot in it, since in the last analysis the three of them would be accountable for everything.

Comrade Mareš announces he went ahead and invited Comrade Voráček who was waiting outside.

Apropos of Voráček, Comrade Hábl wishes to express his misgiving that these teachers might blab.

Comrade Mareš informs them that Comrade Director Voráček has taken severe measures against that contingency.

Comrade Hábl establishes that, all precautions to the contrary notwithstanding, among us everything gets blabbed about, for which reason we ought to decide in good time to pull together.

Comrade Kreperát wants to know nevertheless what it's

all about, why Comrade Hábl sent him a teletyped message that his wife had fallen sick and where she was anyway.

Comrade Hábl explains he knows nothing of the whereabouts of Comrade Kreperát's wife, but he couldn't after all have told him on the teletype that people here were dancing on the ceiling.

Comrade Kreperát wonders why they weren't able to handle a couple of jokers on their own.

Comrade Mareš begs him for the chance to explain that it's not a matter of jokers but a professor at the Pedagogical Institute.

Comrade Kreperát asks whether he'd made activist speeches.

Comrade Hábl reports that the man in question explained yesterday at the faculty meeting that the basic law of physics was invalid and shouldn't be taught any longer.

Comrade Kreperát proposes that the D.A. send him a memo, and that takes care of that.

Comrade Mareš addresses Comrade Kreperát as Rudi and explains that the D.A. has no jurisdiction over laws of physics.

Comrade Kreperát asks if Comrade Mareš has looked into any of this.

Comrade Mareš asks if Comrade Kreperát isn't overtired.

Comrade Kreperát says, they guessed it, he was at an election meeting till midnight, at six he'd gone to his district office, and from there they'd yanked him before lunch, and would they be good enough to tell him what it's all about so he'd be a little the wiser.

Comrade Hábl reads from the dossier: "Juráček, born in K., 33, college degree, non-political, no previous convictions, teaches drawing and physical education at the Pedagogical Institute."

Comrade Kreperát says he knows him, knows him very well indeed, that's the yokel that accused his son of having set fire to the wastebasket during class, and on top of that with a magnifying glass. Comrade Kreperát asks if such a thing has ever been heard of.

Comrade Mareš observes that a factory can be set on fire with a magnifying glass.

Comrade Kreperát says that was understandable at the time of the class war, but why now? Why a wastepaper basket? Anyway, he had given the kid a couple of slaps, the child of some comedian might permit himself to do a thing like that but not the son of Comrade Kreperát. Comrade Kreperát wants to know what's the matter with this Juráček.

Comrade Hábl says that Professor Juráček questions the validity of the law of earth's gravity, namely, that a stone which one lets fall falls.

Comrade Kreperát proposes they lock him up in a nuthouse, and that takes care of that.

Comrade Mareš again addresses Comrade Kreperát as Rudi and draws his attention to the fact that Professor Juráček had after all proved his point by climbing up on the ceiling of the faculty room.

Comrade Kreperát claims this was our old sickness, we had brought about a revolution in farming and flying to the moon and who knows what else, but when it comes to a crackpot intellectual we fall on our ass. Comrade Kreperát asks why haven't we put the director in charge. If this guy teaches gym and drawing, let Voráček tell him not to stick his nose . . . Comrade Kreperát interrupts himself and wants to know what he is to understand by "climbed up."

Comrade Hábl reads: "Professor Juráček climbed to the ceiling of the faculty room and without any outside help, remained stuck to it, head down, as though he were standing on the floor. Only after colleague Sováková fainted did he lower himself and offered her assistance since all the rest of us were frozen."

Comrade Kreperát asks what kind of crap Comrade Hábl was reading.

Comrade Hábl points out it is the report of Comrade Director Voráček.

Comrade Kreperát inquires whether this is supposed to be an April Fool's joke.

Comrade Mareš responds that today is March 5.

Comrade Kreperát proposes to lock up Director Voráček in the nuthouse, and that takes care of that.

Comrade Mareš points out that according to Comrade Voráček's report sixteen members of the faculty witnessed the event. He is of the opinion that Rudi would have to come to terms with it just as he, Comrade Mareš, was trying to do and look at it from a positive angle.

Comrade Kreperát says, hold everything, this isn't right, Comrades, and he asks Comrade Hábl to call in Comrade Voráček.

Comrade Hábl asks Comrade Kreperát if we shouldn't first among us, since he really was of the opinion, in a matter of this sort pulling together was essential, so we wouldn't put our foot in it.

Comrade Kreperát discloses to his comrades that they had already done that, and that they should in due course inform him what their workload was if they could afford to call him in for a thing like this. He has Comrade Voráček come in.

Comrade Voráček appears.

Comrade Kreperát urges his comrade to own up and confess what it's all about. At the Pedagogical Institute—Comrade Kreperát doesn't have to cite documents—people entrust their children to you so that you educate them in the fundamentals of knowledge, Comrade Kreperát doesn't have to emphasize, scientific knowledge of course, so that they will not be misfits but develop everything positive, because the way young people are that's the way the future of K. and our whole country will look. Youth needs a model—a point made more than once by the most competent of voices—and this model begins with the educators, especially those who educate the future educators. And you? Comrade Kreperát would very much like to know if you' ? been tipping the bottle or what? If the very Director of the school fools around like that and with him the entire faculty, then no comrades need be surprised if the more high-spirited students set fire to wastebaskets, yes, they can congratulate themselves that the entire school hasn't gone up in flames.

Comrade Voráček maintains there's no fooling around, he himself was stunned, it was the truth, and he was going to stick to it.

Comrade Kreperát asks, what is the truth, and what was he going to stick to, maybe that a drawing teacher hung from the ceiling like a bat?

Comrade Voráček reiterates, he did so hang.

Comrade Kreperát asks, who had hung him there?

Comrade Voráček reiterates, nobody had hung him there, he'd climbed up himself and without any outside help remained stuck to it, head down, as though he were standing on the floor. Only after Colleague Sováková fainted, did he lower himself and . . .

Comrade Kreperát interrupts him and issues him a warning. We encourage intelligence, we give it room to flourish such as you've never dreamt of, but we don't let it put something over on us. Comrade Kreperát reminds Comrade Voráček that he is only 33 and already Director, which is no accident, because there are many older educators, but Comrade Voráček was expected to toe the line. Comrade Kreperát challenges him to pull himself together and tell us who's calling the tune and what he's really trying to do.

Comrade Nohýnek appears for consultation.

Comrade Nohýnek excuses himself for interrupting but he comes from having examined Vilibald Bláha, who has become involved in the Juráček case.

Comrade Hábl points out that he pointed out that everything gets blabbed about, and therefore we should make up our minds and pull together.

Comrade Kreperát asks what kind of a type he is.

Comrade Voráček replies, he is Professor of Physics at the Pedagogical Institute.

Comrade Kreperát welcomes this news and wants to know if he has confessed.

Comrade Nohýnek asks, what?

Comrade Kreperát invites everyone not to pull the wool over his eyes, it concerned some kind of physical experiment. If sixteen drillmasters are made to pull the wool over the authorities' eyes with the story that people can walk on the ceiling, then there's something behind it, that's as clear as a bottle of air.

Comrade Nohýnek reports that Professor Bláha reported to his office solely as an eyewitness, and proceeds to read the statement of Professor Bláha's examination, see attached. The second part is played on the tape recorder. At the conclusion

Comrade Mareš wants to express the feeling he harbors since Comrade Voráček reported the case, namely, a certain pleasant excitement . . .

Comrade Hábl interrupts Comrade Mareš with the proposal that we should proceed as a three-man board, pull together before pressure can be exerted on us . . .

Comrade Voráček interrupts Comrade Hábl by pleading to Comrade Kreperát to relieve him of his duties as Director, since he cannot, he really cannot, his original fields were Czech and Geography, but nevertheless he believes Comrade Bláha, that is, Comrade Juráček, is right when he maintains that a law once broken is a law no longer.

Comrade Hábl interrupts Comrade Voráček by saying, that's nonsense.

Comrade Voráček interrupts Comrade Hábl by saying, in politics maybe, or perhaps also in jurisprudence, but a law of nature is something else. Comrade Voráček can sympathize with Comrade Bláha if he's going to announce to his students tomorrow that the law of gravity no longer holds, and how is he going to prove it to them theoretically, and what is he going to offer them in its place? On the other hand, if he persists with the accepted law of gravity, and for instance gives low grades, and the students find out that another teacher walks on the ceiling, what are they going to think of Comrade Bláha? Of the Director? Comrade Voráček has students, yes, but we all have children too, and Comrade Voráček would like to know how are we supposed to look them in the eyes?

Comrade Kreperát interrupts all comrades and cautions them to stick to the business at hand. The citizens hadn't elected us to take to our heels when faced with a somewhat complicated problem, at least not Comrade Kreperát. Supposing someone was really walking around on the ceiling, you couldn't begin to handle that with a resignation. Comrade Kreperát recalled tougher fixes, and we had overcome them. If everyone was going to hand in his resignation, there'd never be a revolution. Comrade Kreperát emphasizes that a resignation wouldn't do a thing, we hand in our resignation and he'll go right on parading up and down the ceiling, that's like being given a big fat slap.

Comrade Hábl proposes once again we should first . . .

Comrade Kreperát holds the view that as a three-man board we are in for a sound walloping, that someone in town —while Comrade Hábl is forever pulling together—is going to start a panic, one person has already run to the police, and what if another gets it in tomorrow's paper, and from what he (Comrade Kreperát) knows of Comrade Mareš, he'd be prepared to do it himself. Comrade Kreperát asserts that we are helped neither by the false enthusiasm of Comrade Mareš nor by the defeatism of Comrade Voráček and not by Comrade Hábl's marking time, for we have to face this thing head-on. Let us find out what is actually at issue, what this character is really trying to do, in short, conduct a thorough investigation, and then call in the elected authorities, make short shrift, and that takes care of that. We have decrees, we have laws, so why such qualms, why such hokey-pokey secrecy. Comrade Kreperát concludes with the words that, we here, Comrades, shall put things in order, in school and at home, and he asks who's got his buggy here because his driver is on the road looking for his wife.

Comrade Nohýnek offers him his.

Comrade Kreperát accepts but at once reconsiders because he wouldn't want to ride in a patrol car.

Comrade Nohýnek assures him that the sirens won't have to be turned on.

Comrade Kreperát says, it wouldn't look good anyway, and he would ride with Comrade Hábl.

Comrade Hábl asks, where?

Comrade Kreperát says, to this Juráček, obviously. If I am going to forbid something, I first want to see it.

Proceedings conclude at 3:40 P.M. Comrade Hábl regrets not being able to go along on account of a firm appointment with the dentist. Comrade Kreperát takes Comrade Mareš' car.

[Note: As becomes clear from later documents, namely, Comrade Hábl's address of March 20, same year, his remarks in these minutes are rather slanted; the shorthand transcript discloses that he thinks and speaks in a highly individual manner; that is why his role in the later development of the case becomes far more crucial than appears at this meeting.]

RECONSTRUCTION 3

(According to contemporary records)

When he got into
the taxi, while his colleagues were standing pale and silent and far apart on stairs and hallways of the school each waiting his turn

to leave the building, he felt he couldn't ignore Director Voráček's order and visit Kateřina Horová, even though he wished for nothing better. His hands and feet were suddenly leaden weights as though gravity, which he had escaped twice that day, was going to make up for what it had lost, and was going to assert

the existence denied it, he wasn't even in a condition to relish to the fullest the fact that for the first time, yes, the first time in his life, he was riding a taxi, more: that for the first time in his life he was using any public trans

portation, for when his father was alive, the train conductor, who could claim free tickets for members of his family, he had never been on a trip away from the company apartment above the Lower Station in which on Wednesday, December 24, 19--, he first saw the light of the world, more precisely: the light of

candles. For a long time he thought his father was the neighbor, a pensioner, who

looked after him and his mother, because his real father, the train conductor, had to be on a train on Holy Night which was taken unawares by a snowstorm in Northern Moravia and thanks to an unusually heavy winter was not liberated until

spring, and where would he travel anyway, or to whom, since his parents had only a single living relative, his mother's brother, František Hopner, with whom she had been out of touch ever since her wedding because he refused to give her the cuckoo-clock which she loved above everything, moreover, he lived in the community of Xavírov, at that time a good twenty-one kilometers from the nearest train station, besides he dreamed in

those happy days he spent at the window from which he could watch every movement on the little platform with its

siding, reminding one of a toy train—the arrival and departure times of the railworkers making a deep impression —he dreamed of those happy evenings when he was in charge of working the warning signals and had gone to bed where night after night he took on the job of

stationmaster, dreamed down to the last detail the moment when his young feet would leave for the first time the solid earth, step on two wooden running boards and ascend to the platform of the train, which would take off with him and provide him at last with that ecstasy of movement, fantasied and spiritually experienced a thousand times, that left the body free to give itself with all its strength to further

dreamings, and perhaps, no: certainly, here can be located the embryonic shape of his future achievement. For his imaginary train journey he chose the next round anniversary of the trial run of the world's first locomotive, "The Rocket," invented by George Stephenson, that took place on September 27, 1825, on the Stockton-Darlington section at a speed of 19 kilometers per hour, fully loaded.

At three he secretly learned how to read in order to devour as soon as he was left alone in the apartment of the neighbor, a pensioner, under the pretext of looking after his canary, all the books on railroads, which were the pensioner's

passion, at six he mastered the biography of Pyotr Kozmich Frolov, son of Kozma Dimitrevich Frolov, according to whose design the first Russian horse-drawn railroad was laid in the Altai Mountains from 1806 to 1809, seventeen years earlier than America and thirteen earlier than France, together with the names of the directors and engineers of the Union Pacific, as well as the history of the first railroad section in Bohemia from Píň past Unhošt to the Písek Gate in Prague ceremoniously inaugurated in the year 1830 and in the year 1834

abandoned owing to dearth of building materials. No wonder that after much begging he got his mother to cut him a miniature replica from the discarded uniform of his father, of course behind his back, for his "maiden" voyage, he saved the pennies which his father allowed him for sweet licorice sticks, for ten cents he went out in sleet and snow to get his neighbor, the pensioner, fresh birdseed, nor shall it be concealed that occasionally he made his way to the finer section of town where he did not hesitate to

beg money from the vacationers, all in order to buy himself from his own means a conductor's ticket-punch, shoulder-bag and a

visored cap, he pictured how he would flabbergast his father, the train conductor, and his colleagues and superiors and how he would talk the former in the presence of the latter into not sending him to school but permitting him to work alongside of him.

All this and more came to nothing on that tragic day when his father the conductor, owing to absent-mindness according to the mother, but more the result of excessive indulgence in alcohol according to the railroad authorities, committed his single professional lapse, which not only cost him his company apartment but also

his life, and his wife, widowed from that day, entitled only to a modest pension, found a job as housemaid in the Grand Hotel and took him to an apartment in the center of the resort where one could look from the single window upon nothing but the window opposite hardly an arm's length away. Not only did he cease to speak, but he

pledged never to touch alcohol and never to use a public conveyance as they had both robbed him of his father and his dream. Fortunately soon there was the turmoil of

war and other events, which altered the course of affairs in the world and in K., whose new city fathers quickly redressed social

inequities, being fifteen now he could confidently and easily count on becoming an elevator operator, which his mother very much desired because she hoped that a quiet elevator cab would most effectively counteract his taciturn nature, but then came the summer vacation before his final school year and the fateful encounter with the angelic Kateřina Horová, and the

student for whose promotion to the next higher grade one had had to beg on one's knees, became a paragon. His teacher, who tried to save his former favorites from demotion, pronounced his achievements a fraud and insisted on a second examination supervised by a committee, whereupon he was retired, and the school had its

prodigy, everything that he had read in the apartment of the neighbor, a pensioner, and that he had thought through in the long years of his silence, bubbled forth like the hot mineral waters in the town's pump room, waters which alone were responsible for making K. into a popular

spa. Of course, there was no more talk of an elevator, the perplexed mother was beset with pleas to let her son continue his schooling and her reservations were overcome by means of a respectable stipend. Truly, no one regretted it, for he gave them all the delicious satisfaction of witnessing how the hated

school inspector, who during the matriculation exams had it in for the English teachers, did not understand the student's extensive idiomatic expressions culled predominantly from the First Folio version of Shakespeare's comedies, and had to fake

an epileptic fit, they were dismayed when he picked from the register of all colleges, and all were open to him, the Institute for Physical Education that also offered training in art, for days they tried to talk him into taking a technical subject or languages, but he stuck to his decision, for what did they know of the little platform and siding

that reminded one of a toy train, he wanted to study nothing that would wake in him memories of his ten silent years, but he was instinctively and far more

powerfully attracted by the secret of movement, so finally with heavy heart he was given permission, in the Institute too he was among the best students, helped by staying true to his two pledges, he drank nothing but water and used no vehicle of transportation, not even when he went off to Prague the first time, and whenever he felt the desire to see his mother or Kateřina Horová, he took his little suitcase and

walked, uncounted drivers stopped voluntarily when they caught sight of this gaunt boy in pouring rain or burning sun now hiking towards Prague, now towards

K., drove on shaking their heads, while many a truck-driver spat furiously for having stopped in vain, a single lady in her best years pursued him for twelve kilometers at walking speed and broke into tears when they were separated by a lowered barrier at a railway crossing, into which she

crashed, since which time he made his way across fields whenever possible, after two years he managed the trip between sunrise and

sunset, when that became known the Institute for National Walking Championships nominated him a candidate, but he refused, he refused all competitions on principle, he was threatened with expulsion knowing perfectly well it was a hollow threat, in the classifying heats in the high jump he effortlessly cleared two meters, and he managed to stay under water for 5

minutes and 47.6 seconds, a school record, but unfortunately an unofficial one since the only person with a stop-watch was the instructor, after that he

never again took part in contests:

"I have only one ambition," he said, "that is, to teach my future students to overcome ambition. . . ."

Some mystery was thought to lie behind this assertion, and bit by bit they ceased to pressure him, he took his final examination, packed his little suitcase, and returned by foot to K., where at once he obtained a job at the Pedagogical Institute, at the same time as Voráček, the summer camp torturer of his childhood, who now stood somewhat in awe of him on account of his strangely ascetic

character, he forbade his mother working in the Grand Hotel to carry on the Sisyphean struggle against dirt, looked for a better apartment, making anxiously sure that the windows faced a square which would never be crossed by a regular train, nor a horse-drawn train, nor an electric one, nor a

subway, mornings at the stroke of seven he was off to school, from which he returned for lunch at the stroke of one and dinner at the stroke of six, after which he prepared next day's classes or chatted with his mother and waited patiently until

Kateřina Horová, who was then hardly thirteen, had grown up. Time

passed, and the town had long since forgotten its worst and best student who gradually promised to become its disgrace and ornament, only now and then one of his former professors and present colleagues nodded sadly:

"Juráček, Juráček, never in my life will I understand you. . . ."

But he began to have entirely different concerns, for Kateřina Horová suddenly blossomed, and the deep feelings she always so openly expressed as soon as he made his appearance, in turn, with candy, a doll, a school-bag, ice skates, ski-pants, a sweater, and later with the first item of

cosmetics for the embellishment of her lips, which the saleslady had proposed, to match the redness of his cheeks, for he had the vivid sensation when he bought it that he was engaged in something

indecent—while these feelings did not lessen, they took on different forms,

"Don't cry, I love you, I am going to marry you, then you can beat them all up . . ."

as though something in this sentence had altered, something trivial that nevertheless altered its meaning drastically, as though now it sounded

"I am going to marry you, but *first* you beat them all up . . ."

the more frequently he reminds her that she will soon be done with night school and can at last become his wife, the more often she raises the question of whether he wants forever to remain a run-of-the-mill

Professor of Physical Education and Drawing in K., although he is more talented than the husbands of her sisters, one of whom is already chief caretaker of a morgue, and the second, even more notably of the crematorium, and both had obtained transfers to Prague, together with her sisters at that, while she was still a salesgirl in K. selling

shoes. He had always taken pains to keep their relationship before marriage unsoiled by the carnal, which was not difficult, she knew him literally from the time she had learned to walk, and he believed her emotions for him were such as were unfamiliar even to

Abelard, and that their love for each other was equally worthy of a grave in the cemetery of Père-Lachaise, thus it came about that all the time they spent together was exclusively taken up by

talk, there was something of a crisis when she asked him what kind of a car they were going to buy themselves, only then did he dare tell her the tragic story of his childhood, he anticipated sympathetic understanding, she however broke into tears:

"Because of your stupid pledge am I supposed to spend my life riding around on roller skates . . . ?"

That is what he remembers as he leaves the taxi and for the first time in his life pays a fare, he is too happy and too tired to

fret. The day after their quarrel the young Kreperát had set fire to the wastebasket with his magnifying glass, and

today a new era in the history of mankind had begun, which made old pledges as invalid as old

laws. Dazed he passes his mother, who has written her first

37

letter in thirty-five years to her brother, František Hopner, in Xavírov, in which she forgives him his refusal long ago to let her have the cuckoo-clock, which she loved above everything, a letter in which she coincidentally wishes to pass on the news that threatens to break her lonely

maternal heart, while he asks her in a faint voice not to wake him, he shortly goes to sleep, anxiously watched by her, for nearly twenty-four hours, when there appear in his quarters

Kreperát Senior, Voráček, and Mareš.

ADDRESS

of Comrade Mareš to the plenary session of the town government of K., held on Sunday, March 7, 19--, in the town hall.

(From the stenographic record)

Comrades,

Excuse my agitation but I haven't slept all night. You've known me for twenty years and in all those years have known me to strictly heed every resolution. But the resolution which Comrade Kreperát here proposes—excuse me, Comrade Kreperát—this resolution I cannot accept. (Stirring in the hall.) You have heard the strictly confidential message from Comrade Hábl himself, who left for his dentist right after he finished. I should like to comment that Comrade Hábl is always off to his dentist when important decisions have to be made. In recent days he's been more often at the dentist than at home. (Laughter.) In the interest of truth I must point out it was Comrade Kreperát who called this meeting. The turn proceedings have taken unfortunately raises in me the doubt whether it should have taken place at all. (Comrade Kreperát: "How's that?") When the Director of the Pedagogical Institute, Comrade Voráček, came to me with the matter in question, I instantly realized it was an event of extraordinarily far-reaching implications. I don't want to mention the fact that it took Comrade Hábl several hours before he decided to inform Comrade Kreperát. Comrade Kreperát, truth to tell, left the district office immediately, moreover, it was he who decided that the whole matter be investigated then and there. (Comrade Kreperát: "So what's your beef?") Hold on. Before we got into the car that was to take us to Professor Juráček, Comrade Kreperát declared literally, the words still ring in my ear: "If I am going to forbid something, I first want to see it." Observe, Comrades, Comrade Kreperát did not say "judge," he said "forbid." "If I am going to forbid something." (Comrade Kreperát: "And you were going to permit it? Or what?" Voice in the hall: "Quiet!") Comrade Kreperát, please allow me to finish. So we drove to Professor Juráček's apartment and upon our request, Comrades, he walked on the ceiling (Commotion), and he lay down on it and sat down and stood up again, and, Comrades, he even took Comrade Kreperát's hand and pulled him up. (Uproar in the hall.) Comrade Kreperát can hardly deny that he was mightily impressed, yes indeed, so impressed he didn't ask Professor Juráček, as he had intended, what actually he was really trying to do, he asked him nothing, he wasn't capable of uttering a word, and when we left he didn't even reply to our questions, he went straight across the street into Café Filípek, ordered a triple shot of rum and tipped it down in one gulp. (Comrade Kreperát: "Should I have had them wrap it up?" Voices in the hall: "Don't interrupt.") Thank you, Comrades, for your reminder that discipline also goes for the chairman. I was going to discuss the affair with Comrade Kreperát yesterday, but he couldn't find the time to see me all day. And it was a matter of taking a position in the face of this occurrence, which in the history of this town has not had its equal! (Comrade Kreperát: "That's what the assembly is for." Mild applause.) I didn't want to speak of this, but if you insist, all right: you're a democrat, Rudi, when it suits you, in the district government you kick the assembly around, and then you force on the assembly resolutions you've written yourself. (Uproar in the hall. Comrade Kreperát: "I demand a clarification. What Comrade Mareš says is an insult to the assembly.") Comrade Kreperát, I have never interrupted you, so please don't interrupt me. (Applause.) I don't insult the assembly, I merely claim that you force it to pass resolutions before we've had a chance to familiarize ourselves with every aspect of the issue before us. I don't want to quarrel, I am going to speak plainly. (Voice in the hall: "About time.") Yes, Comrades, it is high time we realized we are standing before a decision whose consequences will be borne not only by our town, but by the entire country, yes, Comrades, by all of mankind. What has actually happened, Comrades? A citizen of our town, known as an upright man and as an exemplary teacher —something I'll come back to later—a fatherless child, helped by our town to a higher education, has paid off his debt by an achievement that places him—I'm no expert, but I dare say—right next to the greatest figures. And what does Comrade Kreperát propose we decide? I quote from the present draft resolution: "One, within the confines of the town all private circus performances are prohibited if they are not approved by the Committee of Cultural Activities, and if they threaten to cause disturbance among the populace. And two, Professor Juráček is to be cautioned not to experiment in fields in which he has no competencies but to devote himself exclusively to his pedagogical duties of physical education and drawing." Comrades, what hypocrisy! (Uproar in the hall. The chairman bangs the gavel.) In one and the same resolution the epoch-making discovery of Professor Juráček is described both as an experiment and a circus attraction. And that is what Comrade Kreperát wishes us to sign. (The chairman again calls for order.) At this point

I can do no better than speak out loud two names, two place names, that should shine for us like red signal beacons—Přímětice and Rybitví, yes, Comrades, Přímětice and Rybitví. (Shouts and questions in the hall.) I'll tell you right away, Comrades. Přímětice near Znojmo is that community in which—permit me to read to you; it doesn't do any harm, Comrade Kreperát, if one doesn't consult one's co-workers, to consult at least an encyclopedia—in which Prokop Diviš, born in Žamberk, North Bohemia, a clergyman, on July 15, 1754, was the first person in the world to attach, although he was equally unqualified for it, a device to the top of a tree to protect buildings from lightning, in short, a so-called lightning-rod. And what did the ignorant, superstitious peasants do? They knocked it down and smashed it to pieces, Comrades. Wasn't that something similar to our resolution? And did that stop lightning-rods from existing? Of course not. It was invented again a hundred and six years later; I repeat, a hundred and six years, namely, by Benjamin Franklin, and therefore the name of Přímětice near Znojmo was not entered in the golden book of progress, but instead it was the American Philadelphia. But that's not all. If we drive home the fact that Prokop Diviš made his invention a hundred and six years before Franklin, we cannot prevent a shiver running down our spines at the thought of what those unenlightened peasants of Přímětice must have on their conscience: how many tragedies and catastrophes took place needlessly, how many lightnings devastated without hindrance our villages and towns. How many conflagrations can be sparked by human idiocy, and not merely local ones, Comrades, we must merely recall what befell our people in those wretched hundred and six years. And that justifies my claim that a direct road leads from that July 15, 1754, out of Přímětice to the place where our independence was buried, Bílá Hora. And if anyone remains unconvinced with the word Přímětice, Comrade Kreperát, it will suffice to mention Rybitví where—I quote again—the cousins Veverka, František

Veverka, coach-builder, and Václav Veverka, smith, invented in the years 1825 to 1827 the moldboard plow which meant a revolution in agriculture. But the community did not allow the moldboard plow to be patented and the invention was appropriated by foreign countries—end of quote. What good did it do them to have a monument ceremoniously unveiled for the cousins back in 1883 in Pardubice? No wonder that the so-called Year of Revolutions, which ploughed up Europe in 1848 and ploughed under so many despotic regimes, left not even one little furrow in our enslaved homeland. (Stirrings in the hall.) We descendants of such a petty, chequered past should slough it off, a past that has tied our hands since the fratricidal battle of Lipany, and that in our decisions today we should deal fairly with a fellow citizen's achievement even though we aren't able to gauge its full dimensions. (Stormy applause.) I repeat, I am no expert, but my heart tells me that something came into being here which will have the same meaning for humanity one day as the invention of the steam engine did or the splitting of the atom. I do not want to anticipate, Comrades, but Comrade Kreperát often calls me an enthusiast. I would immeasurably prefer to be an enthusiast than to become a peasant from Přimětice or an alderman from Rybitví, an enthusiast rather than to rob my hometown or my beloved country of the chance to enter history, or than to—above all—push all of mankind back into the Middle Ages, Comrade Kreperát, because—and with this I will conclude—because our latter-day Galileo punished his rowdy son for setting fire to a wastebasket with a magnifying glass. (The assembly rises and applauds.)

(Note: The address of Comrade Mareš contains a few minor inaccuracies which might confuse younger readers especially. Benjamin Franklin, for instance, discovered the lightning-rod six and not a hundred and six years after Prokop Diviš—as is falsely claimed in the *New Un-*

42

abridged Illustrated Encyclopedia, published in Prague, 1930—so that it is not quite such a case of human stupidity causing conflagrations as Comrade Mareš asserts, and therefore they should not be allowed to overshadow the positive actions of the village proletariat. Similarly, it is most unlikely that a direct road leads from Přímětice to Bílá Hora because although the mentioned burial of our national independence did take place there, it was a hundred and thirty-four years earlier than claimed by Comrade Mareš, namely, in the year 1620, so that the mentioned direct road, if it led anywhere at all, could lead at best only from Bílá Hora to Přímětice.)

RESOLUTION

of the special plenary session of the town government of K., March 7, 19--.

The special plenary session of the town government of K., convened in the town hall on March 7, 19--, under the joint chairmanship of Comrades Hábl, Kreperát, and Mareš, heard extensive and highly confidential testimony by eyewitnesses concerning the conquest of gravity by Comrade Adam Juráček, Professor of Physical Education and Drawing at the Pedagogical Institute in K. After a thorough discussion of the principles related, it was resolved that

(1) inestimably profound gratitude is to be expressed to Comrade Professor Adam Juráček for his unsparing scientific and human endeavors leading to a crowning discovery that promises to liberate our fellow citizens, as well as all progressive mankind, from our very last shackles—the shackles of gravity;

(2) Comrade Professor Adam Juráček is to be requested to carry out most expeditiously theoretical and/or technical elaborations of his discovery with a view to its possible practical and universal application, thereby to explore the feasibility of patenting his discovery before all documentary evidence is submitted to scientific institutions and to higher echelons, and thus to delay the premature publication of the work; until then the entire matter to be kept top secret;

(3) Comrade Voráček, Director of the Pedagogical Institute in K., is instructed to release Comrade Professor Adam Juráček from all teaching duties to give him the requisite time;

(4) Comrade Professor Adam Juráček is to be invited, upon completion of his work, to demonstrate his discovery to the public in person, especially the citizens of K., and then to oversee a more widespread dissemination, particularly among the younger generation. For this purpose the necessary funds are to be made available;

(5) at the same time an art contest is to be announced for the best design of a memorial to the inventor of weightlessness, Comrade Professor Adam Juráček, which should if possible be placed right in the air without a pediment. For this purpose those funds are to be used that will accrue from increased tourism;

(6) Comrade Hábl is instructed, at the next session, to comment on Comrade Professor Adam Juráček's invention and take a position on his activities;

(7) Comrade Kreperát is to be relieved of his present functions and replaced by Comrade Mareš.

All parts of the resolution were voted unanimously.

RECONSTRUCTION 4

(According to contemporary records)

As the historic resolution was being
duplicated, it was stamped "top secret" in accord with
Section 2 of the resolution which meant the document could
be given, against receipt, only to persons marked on the
rating list
VVIP, on which, to be sure, the name of Adam Juráček
never appeared, no wonder that by
March 10, he had no idea what had transpired, he faithfully adhered to his house arrest, looked after his mother,
who got the shivers when the three top officials of the district
and town of K. came to their apartment, and who hadn't
stopped shivering these five days, he cooked as long as the
provisions lasted, read the newspapers of the last three
months, which his mother had had to save in a careful stack
in the small spare room. How it annoyed her
all the years they had lived here, her peasant mentality
refused to grasp what a stack of printed paper was good for,
why it should uselessly take up a room that would have been,
though rather small, big enough for a
washing-machine and mangle. Like every mother, she was
at first little inclined towards her only son's inclination for
Kateřina Horová, she had no way of knowing how vitally the
latter had affected his life and judged her therefore far too
severely, already as a five-year-old she seemed to her too
flirtatious, she advised her son not to wait for her,
"She's too lively for you . . ."
but she had to suffer his standing up to his mother for the
first time and also for the last, she never talked of it again,
and although she never overcame that impression, she made
peace with it. After a while she became even grateful to her,
since the frequent expeditions of her son from Prague to Kateřina Horová in K. meant that she too could enjoy him, she

therefore got used to the idea that the two young people
would marry at the most in

fifteen years, she was, in fact, pleased that grandchildren
would indemnify her for what the lapse of her husband, the
train conductor, had denied her in the way of more children.
She hoped the two would have a good many

sons, in whose raising she would want to play her part, this
is why she growled so fiercely at the newspapers, which she
piled obediently in the small spare room where she pictured
the washing-machine and mangle which had cast their spell
over her back when she worked in the Grand Hotel. She
respected them as the only useful machines in the world in
contrast to

locomotives and train carriages, which she hated for good
reason, as soon as she entered the

spare room with a new bundle of papers, she heard herself
singing by the washing machine and mangle, out of which
miles of diapers were cascading. This scene reconciled her
gradually to the heaviest loss she had endured all her life,
when her brother refused to give her the

cuckoo-clock, beloved by her beyond anything, but they
were all fantasies that in the incredible last months threatened to fade altogether when her son apparently stopped
seeing Kateřina Horová and refused to give her an

explanation, the girl herself appeared in their apartment
one evening before Christmas, asked to see him, but he declined and the mother heeded her son, she spent some time
with her in the kitchen, opened, in fact, a bottle of some kind
of

alcoholic beverage, which she had hidden among the
leaves of a rubber plant, the joyless weeks bringing it about
that she took a sip now and then, while she assured herself
she was honoring the memory of her husband, the train
conductor, how very much she wanted to find out something
from the

girl, but it seemed she was equally lacking the key to the

secret of her son's behavior, it was the first time she felt sorry for the girl and tried to raise in her a little hope, and then she was alone again and continued to pile up the hated newspapers which

now in his house arrest he read one after the other, more precisely, their last and next-to-last pages only, storing in his magnificent memory the names of new artists who enriched the little treasury of national and international artworks, but, above all, the goals, points, and seconds scored in all the latitudes and longitudes. From the

faraway days of looking after the canary he had also acquired an extensive knowledge of this field, another piece of

evidence of his fascination from childhood on in the movement of the human body in all its

forms. The neighbor, a pensioner, had been an active athlete in the workers' organization and had owned, apart from books on railroads, books on this subject too, later

at the Institute they invented a wagering game, called Juroulette, which consisted in the challengers placing a suitable bet and giving Adam Juráček a certain topic, perhaps like

"100-meter and 400-meter records of 1932,"

to which he replied without hesitation,

"Hundred meter, world, Tolan, America, 10.3; national, Engl, 10.6; four hundred meter, world, Carr, America, 46.2; national, Kněnický, 49.5 . . ."

and purely to refresh his memory, as a kind of mental exercise, adding

"Fifteen hundred, world, Ladoumeque, France, 3:49.2; national, Strniště, 4:01.3; five thousand, world, Lehtinen, Finland, 14:17; national, Koščák in 15:14.8 . . ."

the game never lasted long, since they bet exclusively on him, but it was continued in a different form during his examinations, it leaked out that the professors risked large sums, a supposition confirmed by an utterly ransacked savings book found in the pocket of Assistant Professor Bím, who occupied the chair for the high jump and who in the afternoon of the yearly final examination did a

swan dive from the lookout tower of Petřín. It was never officially established, but not once in his life did he read the first and second pages of the paper, moreover, he forgot the very day after examinations the names of even the greatest generals and statesmen, with whom he had made his brilliant reputation since his encounter with the little Kateřina Horová, nor was he able to translate the

morning after his triumphant matriculation the English sentence "I am a student," but of all names he had ever read or heard mentioned, he retained one single one,

Wellington, of whom

he knew just this, that he was a passenger on the first run of the first locomotive in the world, "The Rocket," inventor George Stephenson, date September 27, 1825, Darlington to Stockton, at a speed of 19 kilometers per hour (fully loaded), which was certainly

strange, on the other hand understandable, it was further evidence of how his brain, resembling a perfectly programmed computer, stored only such data as would point to his epoch-making feat, while casting off superfluous

ballast. It caused difficulties when he began his job at K., for as a teacher he was obliged to deliver addresses on the most varied occasions, and the cat was out of the bag when before the end of the school year on the anniversary of Jan Hus' being burned to death he made a speech on the

development of the steam engine, the then Director Baluna was close to threatening dismissal, but his colleague Voráček, as though to make up for the tortures he had devised for his friend in their youth, offered to assume such duties on future occasions, for he had already mastered the names of generals and statesmen better than his own

fields of Czech and Geography. So now he went through the old art reviews, and sports pages, cooked meals from dwindling food supplies, kept adding fuel to the fire that the heat might help cure his mother's shivering, left her two or three times a day for his own room, locked his door, carefully lowered the blinds and stretched himself luxuriously upon the

ceiling, where he thought in turn of Kateřina Horová, the little platform with its siding that reminded one of a

toy train, and the canary, the one silent participant in his doings, thus time passed, until the bell rang, and the postman came with a letter for his mother from her brother František Hopner, who explained that the beloved cuckoo-clock had never worked and so had been sold long ago, and at the same time offered his congratulations. To the question

"for what?" he communicated to them the contents of the top secret solution, in his wife's version, who had got hold of it day before yesterday from the woman who ran a grocery and

fruit store, at which point his mother lost her shivers and, unaware of his astonishment, reached into the rubber plant and pulled from amongst its leaves the bottle of alcohol, the postman instantly doffed his shoulder-bag and sat himself at the table, but

her son didn't want to lose a moment, swiftly removed his pajamas, in which five days ago the leading representatives of K. had surprised him, dressed himself in his dark suit, in which he had taken his final exams, and chose a tie he had refused to discard these twelve years since the then six-year-old Kateřina Horová had bought it for him with money obtained by selling her angelic hair in the park to an anonymous

old man, ah, what pangs that had given him, in his absent-mindedness, manifesting itself every so often and thereby setting the railroad authorities right that the lapse of his father, the train conductor, was not unequivocally owing to drunkenness, he gave his mother

a tip, kissed the
postman

on his forehead and left the house, after passing a little time in the stairway with the ablest of his students, Václav Klokoč, who had heard of the secret resolution from his stepfather, a waiter in the town hall, and who now in great excitement wanted to be the first to interview him, since he thought this would help him with his entrance examination to the School of Journalism. He was

about to refuse, but then remembered that the moment in which Václav Klokoč, unusually talented in all other subjects, had finally been unable to clear a hundred centimeters, was one of those that had significantly affected the germination of his ideas, he responded

modestly to several questions that revealed both the boy's devotion and professional inexperience, then, at the boy's insistence, demonstrated his technique on the ceiling of the corridor, following which, in order not to create any

excessive stir, begged the exhilarated student to find him a taxi, and after a few interminable minutes took his seat next to the driver who fortunately had no inkling of whom he was driving. He gave him

the address of the shoe store in which Kateřina Horová worked and left at the very moment Comrade Mareš' car stopped before the

house, after three days the latter had completed the reorganization of his team and had established the fact that the most vital section of the resolution had not been made known to the individual concerned, which is why he personally had set out to

remedy that.

MEMORANDUM

from the director of the Press Censorship Office, Comrade
Machatý, to the Office of the Head of Government,
March 12, 19--.

An employee of the Press Censorship Office has left with
Comrade Machatý a vetoed feature article which was to have
been published in today's morning edition of the newspaper
"Youth." Some district correspondent named Václav Klokoč
(it has been ascertained that he is not a member of the
Journalists' Union, so manifestly a pseudonym) pretends in
the piece to have had a talk with a professor at the Pedagogical Institute in K., a certain A. Juráček, and claims he witnessed how the above-named overcame gravity. Since the
supposed talk alluded to the town's leadership, Comrade
Machatý's suspicions were aroused, and he got in touch with
the chief official of K., Comrade Mareš, in order to alert him
to the case in question and above-named author. To his
surprise, Comrade Mareš confirmed the statement of the
above-named Klokoč and declared the above-named Juráček had overcome the gravity of the earth in his presence too,
and the case had been discussed by the local organization and
approved. Upon being asked by Comrade Machatý to whom
he had made his report about the above-named case, Comrade Mareš replied incomprehensibly that the officials of K.
did not have the intention of spreading horse manure (his
words!) like the officials in Přímětice and Rybitví, and he was
going to report the case as soon as the conditions were right.
Then he hung up. Comrade Machatý thereupon had himself
connected with the local officials in Přímětice (district
Znojmo) and Rybitví (district Pardubice), who emphatically
denied guilt in any fault and being in any way in touch with
the officials of K. Comrade Machatý draws attention to the
case inasmuch as it may perhaps be appropriate to dispatch

a government investigator to K., to Přimětice, and to Rybitví.

Attested by: Jarošová

FROM THE MEMOIRS

of Comrade Joseph Valouch, former bodyguard of the Head of Government.

(Saturday, March 13, 19--.)

. . . waited near his limousine. I glanced at my stopwatch. He was expected any moment. That's why I opened the door. He used to say: "Time gained, everything gained; that's why I take a daily ride; the seconds lost by a door not opened in time cost our people years."

That's why my father was dismissed. Within a week he was dead of shame and disgrace. Never happened to me. I outlasted ten employers.

It was half past ten. I see it as though it were today. He came running with his briefcase. Down to the second. I quickly hid my stopwatch. In my holster. My gun had long become superfluous. Why carry it? I did my job all right without it. Things had calmed down. None of my premiers died by violence. All were voted out.

He quickly ran to his car. Took his seat smartly. I slammed the door after him. Took my place in front. He gave the chauffeur his order. The car was off. Then something happened. Something that had never happened before. A car swerved into the courtyard. Barred our way.

I reached into my holster. Felt my stopwatch. First time

I ever sweated. Quickly pulled off my shoes. All I'd left was judo. But it wasn't necessary. The car was from our car pool. A member of the government jumped out. Minister of Information.

The premier was furious. He was against anything impromptu. He always kept to his timetable. Expected it of others too. He uttered an obscenity. I'm not going to repeat it. I am writing my memoirs for you. For you, my dear children!

He rolled down his bullet-proof window. He shouted: "What's the matter?" The minister wasn't taken aback. "I have to talk with you. It's extremely important." The premier controlled himself. Maybe he was also a little curious. He knew in what awe he was held. Such a thing wasn't usual. It had to be something serious. He opened the door himself. "You tell me as we ride." We were off again.

The premier asked: "What's up? Your old woman left you? Eaten some crap?" The minister remained serious: "It's about this character. The one who's overcome gravity. At least that's what he claims. The town officials claim it too. Which makes it worse."

"What nonsense are you talking about? All new to me."

"Then read this," and he handed him a piece of paper.

"Why bother me with this? That's what I have people for."

The minister kept his deadpan: "They passed the buck to me."

The premier was annoyed: "Then you take care of it."

"First read it. I want to know how you feel. Look, this is no joke."

So he got him to do it. I watched him. In the rearview mirror, as always. He became visibly embarrassed. Didn't know what to say. Then he proposed furiously: "Pack him off to a psychiatrist."

The minister replied: "I thought of that. I called them up. I didn't want to take off then and there. In order not to inflate it. You know what I mean. There's no stopping it after that.

It'll be in the papers in the morning. Day later headlines all over the world. I've spoken to five people. They all said the same. That there are twenty witnesses. They were all there. And all of one mind. They are supporting him. They passed a resolution."

"Why wasn't this reported to us?"

"They wanted to get it patented first. So it would stay in the country. Apparently it's epoch-making. Now I'll confess something to you. I too think it's great."

The premier had calmed down. He was taken by surprise. But he didn't give up that easy.

"Is it really all that exciting? What's it good for?"

"Great God! Good for, good for? I am no scientist. But I am willing to bet. It's a revolution."

The premier froze. "Wait a minute. Then it really is serious." He switched on his radiophone. Then he spoke into it: "Crow? This is Eagle. I am telling Láda to see you. Cover name? What's your cover name?" he asked the minister.

"Sparrow."

"It's Sparrow. He's going to bring you a nut. Put a team on it. Also I'm going to call the cabinet together. Tonight. This the thirteenth? Then let's just postpone it. Meeting starts at zero-zero-thirteen."

He hung up and said: "Keep after it. Make a study of the thing. What it can give us. And how far it can harm us. Good-bye until tonight. Excuse me for not stopping. I've lost twenty seconds."

The minister understood. He waved his hand behind him. His car approached ours. The minister opened the door. The others did the same. His personal guard. I had recognized him earlier. When they barred our way. That's why I didn't shoot. It was your Uncle Alois. There's an example for you, children.

The minister jumped with precision. He had been a famous clown.

The premier didn't notice. He was already buried in

his papers. More work was waiting. Life doesn't stand
still. . . .

RECONSTRUCTION 5

(According to contemporary records)

As the old
taxi climbed coughing up the steep winding road and
shortly after precipitously descended the street
named after the town, for K. was rather unfortunately cut
off from its resort section, which in the morning could only
be entered by cars marked I.P. (Important Persons), mornings and afternoons by those marked V.I.P. (Very Important
Persons), and by day and night exclusively by those marked
V.V.I.P. (Very Very Important Persons), he was as
excited as
that time many years ago when he had begged for and
obtained that final coin he needed to buy a small ticket-
punch, a shoulder-bag, and a visored cap to complete his
miniature uniform, arriving at the store after the blinds had
been lowered, always too
late, he saw on the table at home the ticket-punch, shoulder-bag, and visored cap, the only property left by his father,
the train conductor, and it seemed to him as though, between
that
episode and the present, centuries had elapsed, and he
exhorted the driver with a hundred-crown note to go faster
in order to reduce the number of seconds that
separated him from her, with whom he associated so many
fateful moments, beginning with the tragic death of her father, who, tired after a night of celebrating, fell asleep in his
plane just before it landed, since which time there was an

ordinance that every plane had to carry at least two

pilots, he always saw her face as it had glowed in the Café Filípek above the ski sweater, which he had knitted her himself as a Christmas present, a skill acquired out of boredom when he lived in the student dormitory while his friends went out on dates, and knitting sometimes on his hikes from Prague to K. and from K. to Prague made time seem shorter, but above all

he saw the tears pouring from her after he had told her they should not see each other for three months, since he had to give all his energies to a certain undertaking, nor did it calm her when he swore there was no other woman involved, she left sadly but that is

how it had to be.

The wastebasket, ignited by the Kreperát boy with a handful of sunbeams, seemed suddenly to illuminate his utterly individual human mission, at that moment he realized exactly what

he was after, and also

why, not merely because at the end of the row of A's on the report card his student Klokoč got year after year there grinned a repulsive D for failing repeatedly to clear one hundred centimeters, but rather that Kateřina Horová should not on account of his pledge have to ride through life on

roller-skates, her simple nature and her poor showing in the natural sciences made him reject the path of complicated calculations, equations, and formulas, which she could hardly have followed anyway, and with a perceptiveness innate in genius chose the simplest technique, besides, he had never thought of himself as a scientist. The only note, evidently in his own hand, discovered upon thorough search through all the books he had borrowed that winter from the Prague University Library, was discovered in Brehm's *Animal Life,* and it stated the quintessence of his plan:

"Man, the intellectually highest developed creature, must

be able to achieve what a stupid fly does. . . ."

However, as for him, he had to chew his way through a mountain of scientific literature. The day before Christmas, immediately after collecting papers on the theory of the flank vault, he once again took the road to Prague, and again by foot, correcting the papers as he

walked, having said good-bye to his weeping mother early in the morning with some kind of excuse and with the request to buy herself this once her own Christmas present which she did that very day by getting the

rubber plant, because he ran part of the way, he reached the University Library before closing time, and bribing the janitor, the nightwatchman, and the librarian he was there from Christmas to New Year's absorbed in study, working without food or sleep a full

two hundred and forty hours, already in the apartment above the small platform with siding, reminding one of a toy

train, when he had incredibly little time to indulge his passion (as he could look after the canary only when the neighbor, a pensioner, left his apartment on his own errands), he learned to read according to the integral technique, that is, to absorb the left and right-hand pages simultaneously, which now

served him, when in the early morning of

December 26, he had finished with the works dealing with nature and also with Greek literature which he had examined with particular care in order to dismiss once and for all the method devised by Daedalus and Icarus, he turned his attention to such insights gained by medical science as dealt with the role of will power in human affairs, whereby he happened upon the word

yoga, which

immediately struck him with great force, he scented a new trail, experienced however another sudden shock when he was given to understand that the entire domestic and European literature on yoga had years ago been dismissed as too idealistic, for two hours he was in a state of utter depression, his need for food, sleep, and home began to reassert themselves when the untiring pump of his longing, which had maintained its pressure even while

depressed, caused a new idea to float to the surface, he asked for all available Indian literature in the

original, to be sure, at first he had to clear the language barrier, and since he had moved into an entirely fresh area, he learned at first, erroneously,

the Prakrit languages, Indian dialects current in the sixth century B.C., so that he mastered Pali-Magadhi, Maharastri, Sauraseni-Magadhi, Paisaci, and Apabhramsa before a lucky accident put him in touch with two students of the Oriental Institute, he stumbled upon their Ph.D. dissertations about Asoka inscriptions, composed in that very dialect of Pali-Magadhi, and the two, delighted that they had been saved at least three months' work, confided to him in return that the most important work on yoga was written in the chronologically later

Sanskrit, so he quickly forgot all Prakrit languages, as he always did when he needed new storage facilities for his mind (once when he had begun teaching physical education and drawing he lost overnight the ability to

write), he made up for lost time by an intensified study of Panini's Sanskrit grammar of the fifth to fourth century B.C., called *Eight Chapters* and written in the sutra style, so that he greeted the new year by opening, deeply moved, the work

Yoga-sutra, whose author, two

hundred years before Christ's birth, was in all probability Patanjali, author also of the *Great Commentary.* He opened the book, and from it there was opened to him a

world, new and yet not unfamiliar, alien and yet close, the world of Brahminism, and yet that of Adam Juráček, a world of meditation and asceticism, so like the inner world of his silent years, spent in the apartment in the center of K. from whose only window one caught the window opposite merely an arm's length away and nothing else, the years he had stopped speaking and confined himself to minimal communication with his mother and teachers, and despite maternal tears and slaps ate no more than his body minimally required for

physical survival, he was promptly caught by the assertion that the feelings, the thinking, and the actions of the human being are determined by two poles, a positive one, whose seat is in the head, the dwelling of Vishnu, and a negative one, whose center is the lowermost vertebra, where coiled like a snake the goddess of nature

Kundalini rules waiting for the propitious moment to rise through the spinal cord to unite with her master, whereby the highest tension and fulfilment occur in the human organism, precisely that state in which he could give reality to his

plan and could do it by a specific training, therefore he concentrated upon it and was met by greatest surprise, after having acquainted himself with Siddhasana, Matsyasana, Padmasana, Trikonasana, Salabhasana, Arda-Salabhasana, Dhanurasana, Mayurasana, Viparita-Karani, and the exceedingly difficult Sirshasana, which amounts to the

meditator kneeling, placing his crossed arms in front of him, throwing his head upon them, and raising his legs straight in the air, it was with surprise then that he discovered they were

the same exercises called for by the curriculum for physical education in primary, secondary, technical schools and universities, that is, so-called

calisthenics, and he felt gratitude towards his neighbor, the pensioner, as well as a thousand others like him who were responsible that through workers' and Sokol athletic clubs, through athletic meets and Spartan Games, calisthenics had taken roots as deep as

beer, forming thus a foundation upon which he could safely construct his technique, without having to fear it would be inaccessible to the

59

masses. This insight struck him on January 2, at 5:55, so that he still had time to return the books, to say good-bye to the janitor, the nightwatchman, and the librarian, who had grown so fond of him that they accompanied him nearly to Pilsen, where he had to leave them exhausted in a ditch, he sent an

ambulance after them and quickened his pace so that at the stroke of eight he entered the gym fresh and rested, then submitted the theory of the flank vault to a

practical test, and that very evening began the crucial stage of his experiments, the stage of concentrating all his mental and physical powers upon one point, the single item he had taken over from Hatha-yoga, completely forgetting all the rest, in order to lower his specific

weight, from this point on he connected to the indigenous ways by taking the positions required for concentration from such exercises as even Václav Klokoč had mastered, for example, the one that called for his stretching himself flat out,

his arms by his side. From six in the evening to six in the morning he lay on his couch, his eyes glued to the ceiling in the attempt to clutch every tiniest irregularity which the brush of the painter had left behind, they had for his experiment the same significance as a narrow ledge has in the

north wall of the Eiger Mountain. He kept this up in school, had long learned how to make his greetings automatic, and his replies mere reflexes, now he learned how to teach by automatic devices, he began to use a tape recorder into which he had already in December and with great foresight dictated the major part of his lectures in drawing and physical education, covering the entire

semester, at the semi-annual faculty meeting Director Voráček singled him out as a pioneer in modern teaching methods, the only occasion in that period on which he

smiled, thanks to the tape recorder he could also concentrate while in class, the tape recorder lectured while he stared at the ceiling maintaining with his heels together the so-called

basic position, he regretted that it hadn't occurred to him to record the examination questions and his responses to the probable answers of each student, but in time not even the examinations distracted him, he attained such a degree of concentration that he no longer needed the tape recorder, he

simply switched an insignificant part of his agile brain to the job of teaching while the far larger share of his thought bank worked on his undertaking, until March 4, when the

ceiling of his room, without forewarning, without a signal, without the least premonition, began to approach until it suddenly turned upside down and held him just as reliably as

the floor had done before, and so he

arrived in the rickety taxi at the familiar shoe store, got out and ran, ignoring the thousand thank-you's of the driver, through the door into the familiar room smelling of

leather and shoe polish, did not even notice the bewildered faces of the sales staff, and when he didn't catch sight of the one he loved in her accustomed place behind the counter, he hurried to the only other place she could be, the room behind a

screen, chock-full with piles of shoe boxes, in the dimness he recognized her outline in front of the window, she turned her back to him as she was rummaging for an odd-sized pair of green suede shoes, the whim of a dandy from the

glass factory, he felt a suffusing faintness, covered the steps remaining between him and the object of his love, embraced her from behind, kissed her hair, she knew him at once, snuggled closer to

him and whispered tenderly:

"My Jiří. . . ."

REMINISCENCE

of Kateřina Katoliková (maiden name, Horová).

I frankly confess I'm pleasantly surprised it was me you turned to. I do, indeed, recall certain matters that are known to me and no one else, and it would have been a lasting pity had they remained cloaked in secrecy. I myself did consider the idea of publishing our private correspondence but unfortunately he never wrote me any letters. I have only two picture postcards from him, one from the Giant Mountains where he was on a skiing vacation with his class, and one from the hospital in K. where he was laid up with jaundice. Alas, both have only my address because he forgot to send me a message. Usually when he had something to tell me, he visited me personally, even if he had to come all the way from Prague. That took less of his time, he said, because according to him he muddled the letters of the alphabet anyway. In the same vein, I recall his mentioning a number of times that he went everywhere on foot, but I took it for a joke. Once we had an argument about it, and I frankly confess that I don't believe him to this day. I don't know whether he loved me though he certainly did hang on to me. I don't want to conceal a certain affection I had for him since childhood. Since the age of two, to be exact, according to him and my departed mother. I cannot confirm it since I personally don't remember. But I do seem to have known him all my life— he took the place of my father, who passed away in an unfortunate airplane accident with twenty-six other passengers. Now and then he brought me small presents, like clothes and shoes. I recall that he often claimed he had made them himself, but I didn't believe that either. When you first met him he gave the impression of being different, nor was it easy to see in him a potential and firm supporter of his life-partner. That is why I followed with growing apprehension his offers of marriage. He referred to some kind of promise of mine of which I have no recollection either. At the same time I was scared by the considerable age difference between us which seemed to be widening from day to day. Nevertheless I was hurt, to confess frankly, when he suddenly declared he'd stop meeting me at six in front of the shoe store next to the post office, nor spend time with me in the evening in the little apartment in Goat Lane, where I lived with my mother, not even take me to a restaurant. No woman appreciates that. In addition he had helped me with my homework for my night course in which I had enrolled in order to get a raise. I frankly confess it went against my grain, and for the first time since we had known each other I permitted myself some rather harsh expressions, which under normal circumstances I would never dream of using since I am by nature shy and was properly brought up. But on this occasion I was convinced they were called for. To my astonishment he remained stubborn and unyieldingly insistent. I recall how I left the restaurant Filípek dissolved in tears, which I however suppressed on the way home in order to avoid gossip. When in fact he didn't show up the next few days I made my way, not without some effort, to the apartment he then had at 1 Park Street, because I didn't want to look for him in school. But his mother wouldn't let me see him. I had met her when we all had gone to a performance of "The Bagpiper of Strakonice." She maintained that she herself wasn't allowed into his room and always had to leave his dinner on a tray outside the door. I recall my shock when a minute later she pulled up some kind of plant under which she had hidden a bottle of vermouth. She poured me one glass while she herself nearly finished the bottle. Throughout, she kept assuring me how her life was a hard one but a necessary sacrifice for her son, and she gave me to understand that she expected the same of me. It all confirmed my suspicion that behind the mystery was another woman. As a consequence, and I frankly confess it, I accepted an hour later the invitation to go to a coffee shop, an invitation made by Mr. Jiří Katolík, whom I met by pure accident on the street. He had been returning to the shoe store several days after buying himself on his first visit a pair of red spats. This went on for about three months, not easy months. Especially because I had to be careful that Mr. Jiří Katolík wouldn't show up in the store too often—not such a simple thing to prevent him from doing seeing I was such a striking beauty. And finally even our store manager, Comrade Kocián, expressed his surprise that it was no longer Adam Juráček who came around but Mr. Katolík instead, who seemed always to be there. So I asked him to have regard for my honor and after that he used to wait for me in a room he had rented while he was making a film in town. That's how it happened that one evening in January I succumbed to him. I frankly confess that I liked him and furthermore he intended to act like a man of honor. Unfortunately when a little bit later my fiancé showed up in the store, I mistook him in the dimness of the back room for Mr. Katolík and addressed him by that name. I recall how he paled to such a degree that he seemed like a light turned on. Then he tried to tell me a tale of how he'd spent his time learning to lift himself into the air, just for me. Of course I didn't believe a single word since I was used to his whims. So I challenged him to give me a sample of his levitational knack. I remember how his stare grew glassy, how his face contorted strangely and turned red, and how he hopped around clumsily without being able to make good his promise. Then I began to laugh at him, not aware he'd been crying. That exasperated me even more, and I told him what I thought, namely, that a man who is a liar and a weakling to boot is not going to be my life-partner. He fainted. I rushed from the store, just as I was, for in no other way could I have avoided scandal. I ran to Jiří Katolík. Luckily he was delighted with the turn events had taken and that same night carried me off to Prague on his motorcycle, remarking that it was anyway his greatest wish that I would bear him a sturdy son since he didn't want to be the last Katolík. It turned out he was only a floodlight operator on the film crew, nevertheless I had nothing to be sorry about. He satisfied all my needs, which is why he died before his time. I have no idea what became of my former fiancé. I was otherwise occupied, bearing my husband eight healthy daughters. They married mostly foreigners, from artistic families alas, despite my objections and qualms that they might end up in reduced circumstances. But true love conquers all. The proof is that I now have twenty-four grandchildren, alas mostly abroad. The only one I have no news from is my fifth daughter, who listened to me and decided to stand on her own two feet after she passed her examinations. In conclusion I want to frankly confess that the years with my former fiancé weren't easy ones and brought me frequent disappointments. Still I am not sorry, because I discovered he was a genius. In order for a man to become a genius, sacrifices have to be made by his nearest and dearest, and that is why Adam Juráček could never have become a genius without those sacrifices of ours.

[Taken down from oral delivery in the Home for Unattached Women in Prague-Smíchov].

RESUMÉ

of the Conjoint Interministerial Commission of the special cabinet meeting of March 14, 19--.

After consultation with scientific experts, it was determined that the events reported from K., in the following designated as the case of EEYORE [a description, clearly for the sake of discretion, was avoided and a covername used from tales and sagas], contradict all basic laws, especially natural laws which do not change and have the same validity in all countries of the most diverse governmental systems.

For that reason it amounts quite unambiguously to a foolish joke, to fraud, or to political provocation.

In any case, upon the request of the Head of Government an inquiry was conducted as to the consequences of EEYORE, should nevertheless something come of it in the future.

The military experts stated that the chief advantage would be the sharp qualitative improvement of the intelligence services and the eventual discontinuance of the production of smaller types of aircraft (reconnaissance, courier, and fighter planes). The danger consisted, on the other hand, in the control of EEYORE falling to countries the populations of which exceed ours.

The experts from the Ministry of the Interior had a similar interest in EEYORE; however, they asked to be guaranteed that it would be in their exclusive charge. A general dissemination, that is, would make the work of the security service considerably more difficult. Above all, intelligent criminals, whose number is continually rising, would obtain an enormous advantage by means of it. Also the supervision of travel abroad would be made practically impossible.

The most negative view was taken by the political experts. The breaking of such a well-known law was liable to shake confidence in laws generally. The representative of the Ministry of Education in particular pointed to the disastrous impression EEYORE would make on the younger generation, especially the students, who were a source of enough worries already.

Recommendation: Reject, and conduct an extensive information campaign. At the same time, initiate proceedings against the instigator.

[Note: Further documents make it clear that the resumé was approved after a debate lasting nearly all night—with the exception of the last paragraph. It was firmly agreed to start the campaign off gradually and keep it low-keyed, emphasizing scientific guidelines and using other than political agencies, in order not to let the case balloon and overshadow more important affairs. One voice opposing, the majority rejected a demand for instituting proceedings since it appeared from the bits of information available so far that the driving force behind EEYORE was seemingly nothing more than naiveté and hometown boosterism. Instead it was decided to dispatch to K., Nauman, Minister of Tourism, who anyway travelled there frequently and wouldn't attract notice, in order to straighten out the local government. In the stenographic record the exact words are "to give them a rubdown and spit in their beer."]

RECONSTRUCTION 6

(According to contemporary records)

When he recovered consciousness an incubus
seemed to be squatting on his chest, and he hoped for a fraction of a second to move it off with a wave of the hand, but what actually oppressed him were a mere few hundred shoe boxes of men's and ladies' shoes which Kateřina Horová had pulled down when she fled, which
fortunately did not escape the sharp eye of manager Kocián who immediately summoned his staff and led an excavation team, when they reached him
he was still breathing. Although the news of his discovery had miraculously not penetrated to them, they outbid one another in expressions of concern, for they were sorry for

him, they detested Jiří Katolík, who stingily bought shoe laces and never anything else, whereas he never visited Kateřina Horová without acquiring at least a pair of children's shoes, which he did out of love for her in order that she should get extra

commission, but they all benefited and that is why Kateřina Horová's two-timing had long since caused them moral disgust, now they offered to call an ambulance and also the

police, but he said no, he was generous, above all, he wanted to save—his heart still reverberated in undiminished force to the old sentence

"Don't cry, I love you, I am going to marry you, and then you can beat them all up . . ."

he wanted to save her name at any price, he tried to convince them he had come to place a large order, so large that Kateřina Horová had shouted in joy and the concurrent air vibration had toppled the stack of shoe boxes, whereupon she had run off in

panic, this idea had come to him from recalling an adventure in the Giant Mountains, he was skiing next to the railroad tracks, overtook a train, and was loudly cheered on by passengers at the windows when he barked a single command which released an avalanche burying two cars, luckily a

thaw had set in at the same time. That they might credit his story, he bought gym shoes for all his students, paid, and finally went out in to the fresh air, which restored him at least to a point at which he could begin to reflect soberly on what had passed, what could be

saved and how, he hurried through the darkening streets, lugging in both arms the packages of gym shoes, driven by a single thought, a premonition, which he must promptly subject to a test. In front of the post office, he encountered a group of his students, they were in the know and began to applaud, they surrounded him and begged him to lift himself off the ground, how gladly he would have complied, but recalling the fiasco in the shoe store, at that before the eyes of Kateřina Horová, gave him the where-withal to refuse, to get rid of the students he began to pass out the gym shoes, in an unwatched moment he dashed off, soon

shook off the last of the students and ran without slowing until a building in *Jugendstil* rose up before him, it was the

station, a small platform with siding that recalled a toy train, my God, how long ago, how much had he buried, suppressed, suffered, and hoped for anew, how much distance covered, an almost ludicrous distance, and by foot at that, in order to come back. He raised his head and caught sight of the window and

behind it his own scrawny face, his child's ears always listening so that the closing of a door would not escape him, the signal that the neighbor, the pensioner, is off on an errand and that the longed-for job of looking after the canary was about to begin. It came to him that a primal

instinct had led him to this place, the very same that compels a murderer to return to the scene of his crime and a wounded animal to creep into its hideout, had led him here where his first

dream was shattered by the news that his father, the train conductor, who throughout his entire life had been the proto-type of a railroad man, a personification of order and punctu-ality, had been guilty of the one lapse in his life costing him nothing less than his life, namely, that owing to his absent-mindedness, as his mother always maintained, or to an exces-sive use of alcohol, as the railroad authorities kept insisting, he—let it be said at last—stepped, while the train was in

full motion, onto a car which he had ordered uncoupled at the last stop. In what depths of his soul did he have to hide himself from the world in order to survive that incident, to heal himself, and to be wakened into life once again by the childish voice of Kateřina Horová, to blossom anew, to let himself be pollinated by a new dream, and to bear fruit, and now he was here

again, and he realized why here and nowhere else, only a few steps from the place where his cradle had stood, he had to determine exactly what had happened, where the interference had occurred and to remove it, or at least convince himself that everything was the way it should be, and swiftly make for Kateřina Horová, or perhaps

not, he would rather not think about it now, he quickly crossed the empty concourse, still remembered exactly the arrival and departure times of the trains, as they were engraved on his mind a quarter of a century ago together with the gestures of the station attendants, he knew that the workers' trains had just left, and the night expresses and milk trains would have their turns later, so he went to the

men's toilet, hesitated a moment as to whether he should stay near the urinals because the room there was larger, however he went into one of the cubicles, locked it carefully, it was humiliating since up to now he had been able to rise without difficulty in a room filled with furniture and a faculty room filled with colleagues without being distracted by anything, but this was a

crisis, he didn't want to take a

chance, he needed just these four white walls. Below the water tank on the wall was a dirty little window which admitted the flashing of neither signals nor stars, still for safety's sake he hung his coat over it, breathed in deeply, calmed himself, and fixed his gaze upon the whitewashed ceiling, sensing ahead of time the brief moment of dizziness, always a sign that he had made a soft

landing, the moment of absolute concentration approached rapidly, nine, eight, seven, six, five, four, three, two, now, he pushed off and

stayed on the dirty

tiles, was still staring with wide open eyes upon the whitewashed ceiling, but its whiteness reminded him only of a death's-head grin, and a word escaped audibly from his lips that had already taken hold in him under the rumbling of the shoe boxes, a word that he did not hand out with the gym shoes during the commotion in front of the post office, nor shake off when he ran to the station, a word that he had discovered earlier, already in the apartment of his neighbor, the pensioner, hidden behind the canary's birdcage, a word the neighbor had used when he explained to his mother why he could not satisfy a certain

request, the sound of the word reminded him of the first three of the first four notes of Beethoven's Victory symphony, which his father the train conductor used to whistle when he went off to work, he had often tried to expunge it from his memory, from which he had expunged major languages without leaving a trace, but the notes persisted and always came up when least expected, the three short notes knocking inside his head like a graveyard

woodpecker, never did he investigate what it meant, and he stopped himself from speaking it out loud, seeking protection in the last primitive belief that something not spoken did not exist, but still it did exist like a time bomb set to go off amidst thousands of winter and spring shoes, three notes reverberated in a symphony orchestra, and his lips repeated them now

"im—po—tent . . ."

and it had ceased to be a word, he had become the word, and with terror he began to realize what that meant, like a madman he started to push himself away from the dirty tiles and hop insanely in the narrow confines, even using his hands for help senselessly until he finally left off and sank exhausted on the toilet seat and he knew he had done with

gravitating, knew that the word had petrified him into a millstone, that he was caught in a net weighted by sandbags like a moored blimp, that he was overwhelmed by it like a conquered nation, and that it would never leave him, he heard the voice of Kateřina Horová, but it was not the sentence that enabled him to spend hundreds of hours working without food, drink and sleep, since it had nourished him, stilled his thirst, and provided him with energy, but a sentence she had pitched into his face in the midst of slippers, shoes, and sneakers:

"No faker and sissy is going to share my bed . . ."

there was nothing he could say to that, nothing with which he could blot it out of consciousness, he was

impotent, and the

witnesses to his discovery would sooner or later modify their words into those of Mrs. Sováková, Professor of Mathematics and Descriptive Geometry:

"Once it seemed to me as though a man walked on the ceiling . . ."

the unfortunate Václav Klokoč would never master once and for all the hundred centimeters, moreover, would never be admitted to the School of Journalism on account of extreme flightiness, he should at least

warn him, but his strength had left him. Continuing to sit at the edge of the seat, he remembered what had occurred to him before he came here, outside, a few steps away from the spot where his cradle had stood, namely the two possibilities which he had had two minutes ago, and now he weighed the single one left him, he knew what

he was going to do, what he had to do, what he could not refrain from doing, nor was permitted to, it was

absurd, depressing, scandalous, irrational, pitiful, ridiculous, cowardly, fantastic, painful, reactionary, tragic, outrageous, vulgar, disgusting, but

to the point, he

rose heavily from the icy bowl, took up his burden and left the place in which he had lost his greatest battle, a bizarre Waterloo in a yard square, he walked

bent, actually physically aware of the weight of his impotence, utterly exhausted, but there was no turning aside, at least in this respect he had no right to turn aside, he walked through the still empty concourse, for the struggle with the angel had hardly taken more than

five minutes, entered a small cozy cafe, reached into his pocket, but when he realized that he had left his coat hanging on the

water tank (he had wanted to shut out signals and stars and now he was going to the punishment for his

sacrilege), he placed the remaining packages of gym shoes on the dirty counter and said to the hunchbacked bartender firmly though quietly:

"A shot of rum for these."

POSITION PAPER

of the Board of the Academy of Sciences, March 17, 19--, regarding the current state of affairs in the field of the natural sciences.

The Board of the Academy of Sciences dealt at a special meeting with the long-envisaged analysis of the problems confronting the natural sciences, which enjoy an increasing interest on the part of the broadest strata of our society.

Modern times, but above all the new social order, have made it possible in our country to give everyone access to education. Modern means of communication bring daily evidence of scientific progress into our homes. Many inhabitants of our planet have succeeded in seeing with their own eyes the far side of the moon's surface, and even the cosmic probes which have penetrated deep into space have failed to record the least signs of the existence of God; on the contrary, they send innumerable proofs to earth that only confirm the validity of present theories and that reassure man that he inhabits a knowable world governed by precise laws.

It would therefore appear that everything was in perfect order, that citizens could confidently devote themselves to work and leisure and scientists to their discoveries. The truth, however, is otherwise. There continually take place minor and major "miracles," again and again there is a piling-up of ugly, and worse than ugly, prophecies, which upset people and compel scientists to abandon their research and explain to adults on TV, radio, and in the press what their children at home, what elementary and high school students could effortlessly account for.

Regrettably it is no cause for particular surprise if now and then "false prophets" are found among even the educated, whose duty it should be to spread science and especially to lead the younger generation to an understanding of it.

One need merely recall, for example, the idealistic hypothesis of the "thermal death" of the universe with which, in the second half of the nineteenth century, the German physicist Rudolf Clausius together with Lord Kelvin struck horror into mankind. Yet it should have been clear to everyone from the very beginning that this hypothesis was based on an unwarranted extrapolation of laws valid for macro-processes as well as for isolated systems found in space, that the validity of the second law of thermodynamics has its "lower" and "upper" limit—the ground of elemental particles and the ground of giant cosmic processes which affect, for example, the general gravity theories—and that, above all, the empiric feasibility exists of massing matter emitted by stars into newly constituted energy-emitting objects, wherein one can discern the most telling and the most generally comprehensible argument against "thermal death."

The "miracles" and "prophecies" served up today do not even reach this level, but rather sink, as in the Middle Ages, to the domain of the irrational, from where—unfortunately often vigorously supported by the church—they haunt the human subconscious in which the dreadful myths of our forbears still resound.

Yes, all these "laws of transcendental phenomena," even though obtained ostensibly by the "power of the intellect," are so pitiful that one cannot even discuss them in concrete terms. If one did, one would most likely provide their inventors with cheap publicity, undoubtedly their aim. It would make more sense to identify such city fathers as are even today ready to organize parades in order that their communities may attain the attribute of being "world-famous."

Not for nothing has our classic poet uttered the sigh: "Jack of Bohemia is forever Jack, even if he breakfasts on oysters."

Nonetheless we consider it our duty to reiterate a few basic facts from the field of physics, that being the science upon which the attention of today's citizen is especially focused.

The founder of modern physics was the Italian natural scientist and thinker Galileo Galilei who conclusively displaced the Aristotelean scholastic conception of nature, the laws of inertia and of the free fall, and the so-called principle of the relativity of motion. It was he who raised mechanics to a science to which later the English physicist Newton could link himself closely; it was he who was the founder of classical mechanics which was of fundamental significance in the formation of mechanical materialism. Newton formulated the concept of absolute space and absolute time and, above all, the law of gravity which theoretically completed the direction taken by a heliocentric orientation and which became the keystone of a unified physical world view.

Newton's law of gravity, therefore, did not come about by accident; it is the culmination of an epoch and the starting point of a new one.

It suffices to mention that this law upholds the general physical theory of movement, space, and time formulated by Albert Einstein and commonly known as the theory of relativity, which stands in a special relationship to us since it partly came into being in Prague.

It is a theory that is most effectively applied to present-day astronomical studies, and in its turn owes much to the quantum theory of physicists Bohr, Heisenberg, and Schrödinger among others, the physical theory of the movement of elemental particles, which led to the recognition of the objective character of (statistical) probability and contingency laws and thus made it possible for the classical conception of determinism to become common knowledge.

It is hoped that from all the preceding it becomes crystal clear to everyone that the law of gravity is today an indispensable component of an unshakable construct from which humanity sets out for the stars.

This law is universally valid, and the well-known state of weightlessness which occurs in outer space or by means of special equipment is solely its product.

If it was ever "overcome," it was only by the aid of motors, hoisting apparatuses or other mechanical devices, which are not lacking among country-fair mountebanks.

All apprehensions that someone might "break" that law and *eo ipso* cause the downfall of the world, are entirely groundless, indeed, ridiculous.

DISCLAIMER

by the National Press Agency, March 18, 19--.

The Position Paper of the Academy of Sciences published yesterday in all daily papers has raised a number of questions to which the NPA wishes to add the following:

For several days now, news has been spreading that a member of the professional staff of the Pedagogical Institute in K. has on various occasions contested Isaac Newton's law of gravity and as proof has maneuvered himself in various rooms in an inverse fashion.

The NPA is empowered to offer these comments:

As the statement by the Academy of Sciences makes evident, even the most recent researches throughout the world in the field of physics and mechanics have yielded no discoveries that have thrown doubt upon Newton's fundamental work. The law of gravity is and remains the foundation upon which modern science rests and which supports a progressive view of the world.

The NPA declares further that the entire case is made up of coincidences, inadvertencies, and misunderstandings and was inflated by people who placed their personal and their hometown interests above those of our society as a whole. Besides, we remember vividly what methods two years ago the officials of K. used in the reorganization of the province when it was decided to make P. the district capital. The voters will certainly want to make known their attitude to this in April of this year.

The teacher who by his unusual athletic feats has occasioned these conjectures and illusions has realized the inappropriateness of his doings and committed himself to provide full explanation of the matter to the assembled student body of the Institute.

The NPA denies in advance all the unfounded rumors possibly evoked by this Disclaimer and takes the view that the whole matter is herewith definitely closed.

BULLETIN

from the Secretariat of the Ministry of Education, March 19, 19--.

In response to the numerous inquiries evoked by yesterday's official Disclaimer by the National Press Agency, the Minister of Education wishes to make it known that guidelines for physics instruction in high schools continue in full force; students will as hitherto continue to be instructed and graded in accordance with authorized textbooks.

The same applies to vocational schools and technical colleges.

Questions for the matriculation examination in physics were set before March 4 of this year, and therefore all apprehensions of alterations are groundless.

Teachers and professors who in any way deviate from the approved guidelines are acting without authority and will be subject to disciplinary action.

PASTORAL LETTER

to Clergy and Believers, issued by the Archepiscopal Chancellery, March 20, 19--.

Brothers in Christ!

We turn to you in the belief that our words will fall upon the fruitful ground of Christian obedience which we owe to God our Lord, to the Holy Church, as well as to the State whose sensible citizens we all are.

It is true that our Savior and Lord, Jesus Christ, performed miracles in his wanderings, as witnesses have passed on to posterity from the pure sources of our faith, the New Testament, especially according to the gospels of St. Matthew, Mark, Luke, and John. Similarly it is true that the Holy Church has recognized other miracles too by means of which the Father, Son and Holy Ghost have repeatedly made their presence known and borne witness to the infinite care bestowed upon their sheep.

However, we remind you that each of these miracles was carefully investigated and admitted only after due approval by the Holy Father.

Our modern age displays an ever-increasing progress in scientific research from which the Holy Church does not shut herself off, in the belief that everything in this world is owing to God, including, for example, physics. To deny this would mean to disavow the essential nature of the teachings of faith. And indeed does not the best proof for this lie in the fact that at the cradle of European natural sciences stood such godfearing men as in the 12th century the Dominican Albert von Bollstädt unquestionably was and in the thirteenth century the Franciscan Roger Bacon?

To account for natural phenomena by means of definitions and laws is in no way opposed to the incomprehensibility of the Almighty; on the contrary, it serves us as further proof that His mercy is infinite.

Most unfortunately, beloved in Christ, we must in deep sorrow realize that among us there dwell a not insignificant number of those who disdain this mercy. At the mere occurrence of a phenomenon for which science has found no explanation, they cry "O miracle!" and thus commit a twofold sin.

Diminishing the value of genuine miracles which in the past the Holy Church investigated and recognized, they threaten at the same time the equilibrium so painfully achieved between the offices of God and the offices of State. One cannot but sympathize with the State, which secures the common good of the people and the increase of their earthly goods, when it regards such acts as unfriendly.

We have assured the national authorities that we disassociate ourselves now and forever from such acts, and we beg you, brothers in Christ, to renew also your vow of Christian obedience.

Recall the words of St. Thomas Aquinas, the fifth teacher of the Holy Church, who wrote that nothing would serve our faith better than common sense.

Let us pray.

To be read at all religious gatherings and devotions beginning Sunday, 21, III, A.D. MCM--.

MEMO

from the Executive Committee of the Association for Physical Education and Athletic Activities, to all Athletic Clubs, March 20, 19--.

The Executive Committee of the Association for Physical Education and Athletic Activities hereby notifies all athletic clubs that all Czechoslovak records in high jump, pole vault, broad jump, and triple jump, which were in force as of December 31, last year, remain in force.

At the same time, the Committee announces that, in the events noted above, only such achievements will be admitted as records this year as have been attained in conventional ways, that is, without the use of intellect.

In all jumping contests in which new records are anticipated the number of umpires in attendance is to be doubled. Contestants who break an existing record have to submit to a psychological examination; should it appear that their I.Q. exceeds the limit to be established by the Ministry of Public Health at the start of the season, they are to be disqualified.

We are using this confidential way of informing you in order not to trumpet it into a public issue and thereby needlessly attract the attention of foreign field and track organizations, because of the danger that they could demand the exclusion of our athletes from international contests.

Long live athletics!

RECONSTRUCTION 7

(According to Contemporary Records)

When on March 10, 19--, at exactly 7 o'clock he had drunk his first shot of rum in the fourth-class café of the Lower Station in K., incidentally, one shot only, a double was refused him by the hunchbacked bartender on the suspicion that the packages of gym shoes were stolen goods, there occurred

something unexpected, he did not get drunk as

one might expect of a fellow being whom on his thirtieth birthday his colleagues had jokingly honored with a case of milk, he could not even succumb to alcoholic poisoning, but

for a moment he wasn't able to see anything. Before he could call for help his vision returned, endowed with an entirely new capacity. It was as though a black-and-white film on the screen of a modern TV set, a film on the theme "From the Deathhouse," had ended and a show in color of a carnival in Havana had begun, it turned out that his

physique, equipped with so many unusual characteristics, reacted to alcohol as though it were hashish, opium, cocaine, marihuana, LSD, and other drugs, or rather, laughing-gas, either, cyclopropane, chloroform, thiopentobarbital, tribromethanol, and other narcotics, for a

merciful relaxation of his higher brain functions took place without being followed by physical and mental exhaustion and a gradual fading of his personality, his distinct personality changed only qualitatively, the first drink of

rum paralyzed all those cells in his brain that held any unpleasant memories or bad news, the ticket-punch, shoulder-bag, and visored cap, the little platform with its siding that reminded one of a toy train, disappeared as though

in a stream of lava, the apartment in the center of town disappeared with the single window facing

the window opposite no more than an arm's length away, the teenagers in the summer camp disappeared who gave him sneezing powder to smell and poured water down a coat sleeve, Director Baluna disappeared never to be seen again who had threatened him with dismissal for linking Jan Hus with a

steam engine, all, all, all that had ever troubled him or disappointed him, from the

quarrel with the Professor of Physics, Vilibald Bláha, to the pointless house arrest to the frightening tumble of the

shoe boxes of all sizes including extra large, and to the fierce defeat on that strange battlefield, where the toilet bowl had dominated like a nameless hut, but, above all, the flood tides of

rum-Lethe engulfed the sight, sound, and sense of the word "impotent" which explains why the

bloated and stubble-chinned hunchback metamorphosed in the wink of an eye into a cherub, the room into a fantasy from *1001 Nights,* and he began to acclaim the grace of the man and the grandiose splendor of a spit-flecked, fourth-class bar in the Lower Station of K. with such an upsurge of euphoria that the old hothead decided to

knock him down with a tapcock, ready to claim, on the

evidence of the stolen gym shoes, he had acted in self-defense. Luckily

at that moment the motor train from the district capital pulled in, he was not likely to know of it since the train had been in operation less than twenty-three years, a

thirsty crowd of workers from the armament plant poured into the bar, the presence of so many witnesses deflected the hunchback's scheme, which is why he tried at least to draw attention to the villain, counting on his insulting them too in his drunken stupor, until they would have no choice but to administer a thorough

thrashing according to all the rules of the art. He pointed him out to them but was in for a surprise when one of them spread his paws in bewilderment and bellowed

"This is the Professor, the Professor Juráček. . . ."

It was the father of Gustav Mára, a onetime equally inept student whom his predecessors had failed three times in physical education, and when Adam Juráček began to teach at the Pedagogical Institute the boy was repeating the same grade for the fourth time, he took pity on him but since he never had recourse to a lie, he instructed him privately in the athletic discipline of

chess, in which without troubling his conscience he gave him an examination and passed him. Mára Junior was this very moment in Copacabana taking part in a Grandmaster Chess Tournament. His

father embraced the beloved teacher whose photo had found a place in his album next to portraits of statesmen and St. Florian, and although the elder Mára was not a firefighter, yet he was in the habit of quenching his thirst so often and so copiously that he really needed the saint's assistance, now the opportunity presented itself to quench thirst and love with one gulp, but before he

had his chance to order two shots of rum, another fellow who had watched them closely said to some men nearby in a low voice laced with awe:

"That's the one what can walk up on the ceiling . . ."

and it was no longer Mára alone who yearned for the company of the young man whose fame had spread so rapidly thanks to the secret resolution, they all gathered about him and slapped him on his back with rough tenderness, they were highly skilled workers used to handling complicated machinery and they knew how to value

brains that thought up such machines and also thought up other things, things that save physical energy, they knew better than those who made speeches on the subject and passed resolutions what

gravity is, it left its mark on their fingers and palms, it had a permanent entry visa into their muscles, it was their arch enemy, one of the worst, and now this skinny little schoolteacher who looked as though he couldn't tear a

noodle in two, had defeated it and wants to leave them his discovery or at least to their children and grandchildren, and he's one of ours to boot, a fellow countryman, a man from this region in fact, one of our very own, they felt but could not express in words, that is why each of them bought him at least

one shot of rum, with each

glass the world enveloping him became more colorful and more melodious, he didn't know most of them, had never met them, would have sworn, however, they were his very own brothers, concealed from him by his mother and now sent to him directly from heaven, he embraced them, sang with them, signed picture postcards for them which they were going to send to long-forgotten relatives and acquaintances, the place was as though sold out until

summer. The hunchback bartender, having begged forgiveness a hundred times, still knew of customers who drank like pigs with far worse reason than this one must have, desired something special and so brought him his identity card

to sign. Night expresses and milk trains were arriving,

things had to come to an end, not because they were going to be kicked out but because there was nothing left to drink, the bartender wanted to keep them at any price, he even unlocked the medicine chest, but the rubbing alcohol did not last long, they wanted more, someone proposed "The Vulture" where they served Myslivecká, that is, hunter's brew, the hunchback implored them to return when the other place closed, he promised to have new supplies on hand, he hurried off to wake the stationmaster to borrow his

buggy, singing they marched off to "The Vulture," the patrol car with the flasher blinking and blocking their way they simply lifted to their shoulders and took it along explaining to the occupants they were going to use it as a ramrod in case "The Vulture" wouldn't open its doors, the driver honked desperately three short, three long, three short, they only let the patrol go on the promise not to follow them, the promise was

kept, the municipal police force was not equipped to deal with such a battalion of drunks, anyway, they had found out what was being celebrated and were also apprised of the secret resolution. "The Vulture" naturally received the procession like prodigal sons, so did "Korbian's," "The Slipper," "The Balloon," "In the Arcade," "The Embassy," "The Elephant," "The Queen," and "Filípck," where they thought they'd bid their guest of honor good night since his sleeping quarters were right across the street, but he

refused to go to bed. He had learned to drink rum, vodka, cognac, whiskey, aperitif, liqueur, beer, wine, and champagne, he had made the acquaintance of cocktails, highballs, and fizzes, but nowhere was to be found

Myslivecká, that is, hunter's brew, which is why they marched back in the direction of the station, he sent his mother a telegram saying he was o.k., he was thinking of her and would make up for everything at Christmas, they were waiting for him in the saloon until he got back so he could personally tap the barrel. Myslivecká, that is, hunter's brew, did it to him, he abandoned all other drinks and stayed with that, the buggy lugged it in twice daily, he established his headquarters in the station, which was an advantage for everyone, they travelled unceremoniously from the barrel to work and from work to the barrel, no one was surprised by the sudden invasion

of spring, they looked upon it as a direct consequence of his achievement, it was an unconditional surrender of vanquished nature. To save time, they rolled the barrels right on to the small platform near the siding that

reminded him of nothing, he was utterly happy, he did not even notice that the company changed, especially in the morning a group assembled whose members were leery of work, they were lured from the entire district as the spring breezes wafted the aroma of Myslivecká, that is, hunter's brew, to them, however, they were not the ones to buy him drinks, they weren't born yesterday, they were convinced he had

dough, plenty of dough, they thought that the parcels which he kept holding on to, contained the drawings of his invention, they talked it over and offered him a substantial sum for the parcels, he was surprised but sold the lot to them nevertheless, they almost cried with rage but knew which side their bread was buttered on and forced him to sign every single one of the

gym shoes, they in turn peddled them on the streets, it was a gold mine. When he had drunk away what he had earned by this deal, they began to lend him money at interest since the rumor spread he was going to get a national

award and also the Nobel

prize, it had been going on like this for a week, and he did not notice in his intoxication that there were fewer and fewer faces from the first days, that the number of hangers-on rapidly diminished, that more and more often his drinking pals lounged around the concourse, newspapers in their hands, that among them violent arguments broke out and that they more and more frequently asked him a question, which in the first days had never been put to him, namely whether

he could really take a walk on the ceiling, and if so, he should give them a demonstration then and there. He tried to drink more seriously, he sat directly beneath a small barrel and sucked his favorite beverage through a thin rubber hose, when they pressed him, he replied with a shrug: "Leave me alone, I haven't got the time," but he was playing his last chip, even the best aircraft has a precise range, even the strongest physique its maximum load limit, when all is said and done, though he was a genius, he was no

god, in ten days he had drunk as much liquor as a practicing alcoholic consumes in a lifetime, not that he collapsed, much worse: he had

become used to it, the blockage

of his higher brain functions began at first gradually and then more rapidly to let go, so that on the evening of March 20, he caught sight in the doorway of the familiar, longed-for, nearly attained but irrevocably lost

visored cap, and he broke into tears. Everything

returned, absolutely everything, beginning with the window in the center of town from which one faced the opposite window only one arm's length

away, to the coat, with which in an attack of crazed pride he had wanted to shut out the stars and signals while on the battlefield of the men's toilet, it all returned like a boomerang, he remained

alone, in the abandoned spit-flecked fourth-class bar of the Lower Station of K., alone with the bloated hunchback, who crudely informed him he was going to close up, then asked him for the prompt cash payment of twenty-one thousand five hundred and twelve crowns and forty

cents, while he had neither cash nor savings, nor his achievement, nor Kateřina

Horová, at which point there came into the saloon, accompanied by the stationmaster, Comrades Hábl, Voráček and an unfamiliar person who looked like Adolph Menjou who however introduced himself as Minister of
Tourism,
Nauman.

ADDRESS

of Comrade Hábl to the plenary session of the town government of K., convened on Saturday, March 20, 19--, in the town hall.

(Transcribed from the tape recording.)

Comrades,
　You all know me, you know me, you've known me a good twenty years and know, all of you know, know that I have always in a disciplined way, have carried out every single resolution in a disciplined way. But the resolution which here, which you here passed at the session, the unfortunate session, that very unfortunate session of March 7, that resolution, forgive me, Comrades, forgive me, Comrade Mareš, because it was you, you were the one who proposed this resolution, this unfortunate resolution, this resolution I cannot, with the best will in the world, I cannot carry out this resolution. You have all heard, we have heard, we've all heard the information, confidential information, I emphasize this, I stress this from experience, the strictly secret information from Comrade Minister Nauman himself, the Comrade Minister of Tourism. I wasn't present when this resolution,

this unfortunate resolution, was passed, because I was, Comrades, yes, I was, Comrade Mareš, was at the dentist, which seems, seems to many ridiculous, but it is, as it appears, it is good, Comrades, occasionally it is good, Comrade Mareš, occasionally it is good to go to the dentist, because today, today not only my teeth are clean, Comrade Mareš, but both my teeth and my conscience are clean. Could I have, could I have stayed, could I have stayed here with you during that unfortunate session on March 7, stayed with you to the end, I would have, of course, I would have repeated, I would have been merely able to repeat to you what I said at the meeting, the meeting of March 5, said to you, Comrade Mareš, to you and to Comrade Kreperát, said to both of you, it's in the minutes, I said and I'm quoting: "I find we ought to agree upon some kind of a line, a common point-of-view, which we can adhere to when having to face up to both higher and lower echelons, in order not to put our foot in it, since in the last analysis we would be accountable." That's what, Comrades, what I said, said to the comrades, because this affair, I said, we should first the three of us, first as a three-man board, this whole affair from the beginning seemed to me, not to call the assembly, before we had thrashed out, as long as we hadn't ourselves. To be sure, Comrade Kreperát, Comrade Kreperát in his well-known, which is, in his well-known rashness, which is well-known to us, convened, and Comrade Mareš, Comrades, and Comrade Kreperát immediately convened, and Comrade Mareš has this, this persuasiveness, addressed this assembly with his, he knows how, his stirring address to the assembly which caused, we know, what, we all know very well, that unfortunate, and now we are, and we carry, we are there, the responsibility, all of us, we are there, as we are here where we are, Comrades, and where we didn't want to be. I don't want to, I won't make a long, Comrade Nauman, the Comrade Minister has already said, and I have no, and why anyway, Comrades, intention, as we know, each one of us knows, we've seen with our own eyes, we witnessed, what here occurred. And I will tell you, I will tell how I, the way I, tell you what I think. An abuse, we've seen here, a grave abuse, we've seen a grave abuse perpetrated, grave difficulties, in short, difficulties have arisen on account of gravity. (Applause.) We have been through, you too, Comrade Mareš, all kinds of, I am thinking of scenes, Comrades, and such, we all I hope drink, we drink at times a glass, but everything has, I say everything, there are certain, we don't overstep limits. As truly said, and also in the papers, by Comrade Minister, as Comrade Nauman said, and we've read it, each one of us, Comrade Mareš who reads, some prefer encyclopedias, but for myself, sometimes it's o.k., and of primary, primary use, to follow, because the daily press has a series, not just one article, the Academy wrote, the Ministry wrote, and others have also written, the papers are full of it. I was, we all were, most of us, look for yourself, at Filípek's, we know the café, also Comrade Mareš, and you too, that's no longer, doesn't look like a café, that is, if you permit me, I am no, none of us is, the church has her place, her assigned, her precisely assigned place in our society, if anyone, should he believe, but no one can tell us, because that's where he lives, because that's where Professor Jurá-ček, but nobody can, no one has the right, out of a café, a public operation, no right to make a place of pilgrimage out of it, there are candles there, there sit, I honor them, we all honor them, we are all going to be old one day, but these old candle-clutching women, sitting there, silent, absolutely silent about, ask the one in charge, it hits us, and with justice, he sells only sodawater, there they sit and, Comrades, wait until this Juráček, we are, intelligence is, can't deny it, necessary, but Professor Juráček, they're all waiting there, they wait, maybe he'll do it, and we know they're against it, the church itself against it, that he'll perform a miracle. And he, that's well known, only too well known, performs them, but elsewhere, performs miracles of a binge, which we, and I'll stick to that, Comrades, which we never, which none of us has use for. (Applause.) And that, all of that, all because of that unfortunate, to our wives, we have some, me too, because my daughter, we all have, I have seen it myself, the student newspaper, let them, by all means let them publish it, but, here I have it, but that's how far it's gone, here is the article, the headline of the article, I quote, Comrades, and that, I stress, comes from a school with girls, I quote: "How to Get Rid of Body Weight." (Laughter.) No, Comrades, that isn't, it is maybe, but isn't really a laughing matter, actually, or rather, and you feel it, we all feel it, even Comrade Mareš, a crying matter. I shall not, Comrades, I think it is, we feel it, pointless to indulge in polemics, going back, to deal with your speech, Comrade Mareš, your presentation at that time, your unfortunate, I think you should, everyone feels it, all of us, was, forgive me, but it's so, you with your Přímýtice, ridiculous, and Rybitví, ridiculous and dangerous, nowadays, in our time, Comrades, we don't need to, conditions, have any fears that anything, any idea, any true idea, don't need any, will be wiped out, rather, as Comrade Mareš, as was shown, I don't want to, it's not my way, because I was, you realize it, not present, you succeeded, at the dentist, this Diviš of yours, Comrade Mareš, this lightning rod, that is now, as his presence shows, proves and witnesses, the fact he's present, that Comrade Minister, Comrade Nauman sits among us, Comrade Nauman of Tourism, proves that we, Comrade Mareš, this plough of yours, that we now, Comrades, have this plough hanging round our necks. (Applause.) And so I want to, like Comrade Kreperát, want to end, I would rather, like him, Comrades, my own way, as he told me, rather, following Comrade Kreperát, mark time, for a while, it's understood, mark time, until I, as Comrade Nauman, who puts us right, as I run off half-cocked, like the unfortunate, and then you, Comrade Mareš, in disgrace and dishonor, all of us, and me too, return in disgrace and dishonor. (Applause.)

RESOLUTION

**of the special plenary session of the town government of K.,
March 20, 19--.**

The special plenary session of the town government of K.,
which took place on March 20, 19--, under the joint chairmanship of Comrades Mareš and Hábl in the town hall,
heard an extensive as well as strictly confidental report by
Comrade Minister of Tourism, Comrade Nauman, concerning several new aspects related to the so-called overcoming
of the earth's gravity by Adam Juráček, at present Professor
of Physical Education and Drawing at the Pedagogical Institute in K. After a discussion that was short but therefore
dwelt all the more on principles, it was decided:
(1) to pass censure on Adam Juráček with all the attendant
consequences, and on his accomplices who maneuvered the
educational and urban bodies into proceedings which both
violate objectively ascertainable facts embodied in the hitherto valid law of I. Newton, and also the normal common
sense of the overwhelming majority of the working population of K. and the entire district of K.;
(2) Adam Juráček is ordered to confine himself to instructing
the students of the Pedagogical Institute in physical education and drawing and no longer to concern himself with
experiments for which he lacks the required qualifications;
(3) the director of the Pedagogical Institute in K., Comrade
Voráček, is enjoined, for this purpose, to increase the number
of class hours in physical education and drawing, and furthermore, to report to the town government every other day
how the Bulletin of the Ministry of Education of March 19,
this year, is being implemented, especially the final paragraph;
(4) Adam Juráček is emphatically ordered to retract publicly
his claims at a public meeting of the citizens and youth of K.,

as promised in the Disclaimer of the NPA of March 18. On that occasion he is to denounce all the excesses connected with his doings for which he is demonstrably responsible. For this purpose the ballroom of the Grand Hotel is to be reserved for the morning of March 21;

(5) The funds already available are to be expanded on an art contest for the best design of a memorial to the great I. Newton, the discoverer of gravity. The designs are to put special stress upon the weight with which the memorial is to rest solidly upon the pediment.

(6) Comrade Voráček is instructed, at the next meeting, to comment on the affair of his subordinate and friend, Adam Juráček, and take a position on his activities

(7) Comrade Mareš is to be relieved of his present functions and replaced by Comrade Hábl.

All parts of the resolution were voted unanimously.

CONFIDENTIAL REPORT

from Čcnčk Nauman, Minister of Tourism, to the Head of Government, March 20, 19--.

(Delivered by courier.)

Most Honored Comrade Chairman, dear Píd'a,
[Note: The reference is presumably to a nickname from childhood.]

I should like to inform you that I have carried out to the letter the task the government and you personally set me. The finale is all that's left. But I won't take part in it since our exaggerated interest would magnify the affair's importance more than this operetta deserves. The rubdown you ordered for the local gentry I administered first this morning at a roundtable and then at a shindig attended by a hundred local heirs apparent. The spitting into their beer, which was to follow my lead-off dance, they took care of themselves. Instead of this thickheaded Mareš who replaced Kreperát two weeks ago (incidentally, they consider this the only ray of light in the entire mess, they all agree Kreperát would have bossed them another twenty years since he had something on everyone. Nice, eh?), Hábl was picked, no shining light, but at least an honest, experienced, sensitive, devoted, loyal, and, above all, a thoughtful older official, who'd rather check and recheck a dozen times before he does any cutting. Truth is, nothing like this has ever happened to him before (with generous assistance from the dentists to whom he rushes every time a ticklish vote comes up. Something, no? He must be at least on his fifth set of dentures), so that he seems to be really the right man for the given moment, although, again, he is unpopular, officious, nosy, limited, and stupid. (To listen to his address was hellish, as a failed philologist I glanced into the transcript with rapture—fabulous! If I were to compare it with anything—as a failed medical student: a permanent, mental coitus interruptus.) The upstanding Marešites departed when Mareš did, and so the remaining Kreperátists. The spitting into their beer surpassed all expectations, you would have been delighted. Only a single, sole individual survived the past and present session, a certain Nohýnek, responsible for the defense and security section. (By the way, they say of him, he says it of himself, he won't fall unless you fall, since you're supposedly afraid of him, he could mention a tidbit about some bunnies. A joker, eh? I tell everyone here that I have never in my life met you hunting, shouldn't you drown him and his bunnies once and for all?) With Hábl and Voráček (the director of the Pedagogical Institute, such an assiduous cipher, but in the company of a somebody becomes a 10) I went personally to the station to pay my respects to this superfool in a village opera. No, he wasn't going to beat it, he's been hitting the bottle for ten days and has run up a bill for twenty thousand. Thorough, eh? If you're thinking of a muscleman, an Atlas, or the reverse, a prophet or martyr—no luck. An ordinary, average, banal, ready-to-wear type, a trace too thin. As a failed actor I'd say: Orgon from *Tartuffe,* a total nothing, a washrag, piece of dough, jelly, aspic, gelatine, muck. I was prepared to fork out, worst come to worst, the twenty thou, but it didn't even come to it, he gave up like that. Actually he didn't utter one sensible word all that time, he nodded to everything, I had the impression he wished for nothing better than to retract the works. I've got to confess to you, I couldn't resist, as a failed athlete I was all excited, and I begged him to put on his show. He declined as though he'd been asked to rape his mother. He shook and made incomprehensible noises. Same with his refusal when I asked him to write up a speech that I could read first. Instead, he spontaneously volunteered to read a speech someone would write for him. I entrusted this to Voráček because Hábl doesn't look as though he knew how to write. This Voráček had earlier announced he had been present twice while the other ungravitated himself, but as a failed psychologist I know asking him can't do any harm, on the contrary, it'll juice it up. As to the rest, I have lassoed for the last act of my guest performance all those who proclaimed the same heresy. (It's a matter of altogether sixteen professors of the Pedagogical Institute, as well as Kreperát and Mareš, who are so shaken up by their downfall they'd deny anything under the sun, most of all Hábl.) At first this teaching crew wouldn't budge an inch, but then a certain Sováková, a math majorette, explained what bothered her since the event, namely, that she'd imagined it all, and the rest of them obligingly concurred. (Naturally I had the rascals give it to me in writing.) Surprisingly, there was one who did not back down, a certain Vilibald Bláha, a physics professor no less.

I was near despair when this smart-ass Nohýnek whispered to me it was this very Bláha who first reported him. As a failed lawyer I accused him of being a malcontent, whereupon he began to blubber. It was easy going after that. True, he didn't want to sign, but he proposed a trip to Bardějov (ostensibly to ask his former wife for forgiveness! Cute, eh?) We immediately packed him into Hábl's car and sent him off, free of charge, and would you please get Dumpling [Note: This is manifestly the nickname of the lady Minister of Education.] to transfer him right away to that town, preferably to a school for retarded children. (Is physics taught there? If not, let him be called to military duty. To the paratroopers! As a failed officer I daresay that's where he'll soonest find out about gravity, all he'll have to do is not fold his parachute right. I also thought this would be the perfect solution for Juráček, but they told me he was rejected for being physically unfit. A smarty-pants, eh?) For the moment, we've fed him hexobarbitol and quartered him for the night in the Grand Hotel so he should have recovered by morning and remain under guard for his own safety. That's the end of the show, and I'm off for a glass of beer. Tomorrow morning at seven I'll go with the manager of the Grand to hunt boars. (I hope, as a failed veterinarian, to get myself, by pure mistake of course, a wild sow, so that that Nohýnek has as much on me as he does on you. Then we can give him a united boot in the ass.) Ciao.

P.S. This very moment I prevented a slithery catastrophe. I asked to see the speech the worthy Comrade Hábl had composed for tomorrow and as a failed priest I came within a hair's breadth of crossing myself. The suspicion which I had begun to form during his earlier performance was confirmed. His text is crawling with figures which prove that in the district the birthrate keeps dropping and Juráček is being accused that by overcoming gravity he practically wanted to introduce an illegal interruption of pregnancy. The excellent man mixed up gravity and gravidity! Delicious, eh? I have arranged for the guilt-plagued Voráček to write his speech too. With which I close at last and slip away.

Your
Maňýa

[Note: The concluding flourish as well as other places here and there in this confidential report evince an obvious admixture of humor.]

RECONSTRUCTION 8

(According to contemporary records)

When they came to

get him, always in three's, this time the mixture was Hábl, unavoidably Director Voráček, and a doctor, originally the third was to have been Nohýnck, but he excused himself at the last minute because he urgently had to go to—Comrade Hábl would surely understand—

the dental clinic, Comrade Hábl remarked sympathetically it must be unpleasant to have a real toothache. Let it be known that whenever nothing was the matter they used Dr. Hudec, the Head Resident of Internal Medicine at the Polyclinic of K., Comrade Hábl had

appeared, by the way, while it was still night, when they now came into his room, Comrade Hábl possessed the only key to the padlock attached to the door of room No. 157, he was still sleeping, or to put it more precisely, he had just fallen asleep, he had slept a bare two

minutes, had they come a minute sooner they would have discovered on his face the same expression as on the picture above his bed which showed a darling, fat, stark naked child surrounded by tall flowers, for hardly had he fallen asleep than he dreamt of

the small platform with the siding, reminding one of a toy train, he had just returned from the store where they sold him a small ticket-punch, a shoulder-bag, and a visored cap, at a discount even, so that in all decency he could return a part of the money begged from the vacationers. He put on the miniature uniform, which his mother had lovingly sewn for him, which is why it was no

wonder that he actually dumbfounded his father, the train conductor in company with colleagues and superiors and talked him easily into not sending him to school but to permit him to work at his side instead, but they

came one minute later, when the childish smile had given way to genuine terror, for he had just opened the connecting door and stepped, while the train was in motion, into the carriage which at the last stop he had ordered uncoupled, he realized that it was a matter of an inherited

disease, and since he had never enjoyed a drop of alcohol, he just had time to curse the railroad authorities, then sank in an unending free fall towards the rails whisking past, becoming painfully aware that he had forfeited his wonderful achievement, which alone could have

saved him. He cried out and Dr. Hudec rushed to the bed with the worst premonition to which the past night had fully entitled him when they woke him up violently because the closely watched guest in room No. 157 who couldn't fall asleep for anything in the world, although that is what he most fervently desired in order to escape thereby for a few hours his shame and misery and, more than anything, the agonizing thought where, with

whom and how Kateřina Horová was spending the night, this guest had begged each housemaid of the Grand Hotel in turn for sleeping pills, until they got together and realized he had swallowed in all

sixty-seven, alarmed they ran to report to the night manager, who immediately cut short the sleep of the Minister of Tourism, who chased Comrade Hábl from his bed, while Dr. Hudec awoke when someone unkindly pulled Hábl's youngest daughter from his arms, it was

Comrade Hábl himself, but in the excitement he luckily did not recognize his own daughter, whom he had given permission, never granted before, to celebrate his promotion by going skiing that weekend in the company of absolutely sterling girl friends. He addressed her as Comrade Hudec, forgetting entirely that for twenty years the Head Resident had been a

widower, because when smashing through the door he had lost his breath and supported himself, in fact, upon the skis

of his daughter leaning against their bed. He pulled the Head Resident into the other room, not letting him put on more than the pajama halves scattered around the floor, in front of the house

a truck was waiting into which the night staff was loading all the necessary equipment, for Comrade Hábl demanded that the treatment be administered in the

hotel, he wasn't going to take any chance whatsoever, convinced his charge was determined to take his life and therefore capable of anything, the equipment was set up directly beneath the inconceivably fat cherub surrounded by tall flowers, and Head Resident Hudec, for safety's sake, pumped out the valuable stomach

twice, putting into his movements an energy which, were it not for the patient, he would have put to work elsewhere had his scheme prospered, that is why it happened that the effect of the sleeping pills, which were just about to do the job,

was interrupted, and he felt hunger which no one thought of doing anything about because Comrade Hábl in the meantime ordered bars to be attached to the windows and a padlock to the door, he yanked

the telephone out and let the man he had saved know that

he'd just as soon send him to sleep himself, and as a matter of fact began to sing him lullabies while standing beside the bed, unfortunately out of tune, so that Adam Juráček who not surprisingly had absolute

pitch, began to pretend sleep, but he stayed awake in moping loneliness which depressed him no less, while Comrade Hábl had them push two easy chairs in front of the door and got the Head Resident to keep watch with him without suspecting that he thereby preserved for all time the virginity of his favorite daughter, who had not succumbed to the Head Resident the evening before, at least not

entirely, and now that she had glimpsed a higher power intervening in the affair, she made that very spring night her pilgrimage to the mountains, barefoot and carrying her skis like a cross, offering God the gift of an innocence so miraculously saved, the Head Resident

suspected something like this and would if possible have got drunk, if Comrade Hábl had not warned him he'd have his stomach pumped too. So the night passed, with Director Voráček driving himself to undo his mistakes by ceaselessly refining the two drafts, he worried whether he was adequately reproducing the traits and expressions of two such disparate

characters, Adam Juráček's case being a hard nut to crack, but Comrade Hábl's an ineffable work of art, as here the dramatist had hardly

a hundred words at his disposal. Failing hour after hour, he experienced a glorious moment at dawn, such a moment as he had tasted for the first and last time when the then notorious Don Juan of the senior class, shortly before the final examination, could boast of his lady teacher

succumbing to him, whom, more's the pity, he had to marry however, because such an extraordinary success was not without its ordinary consequences, now she was sleeping in the bedroom next to him, gathering strength to protect him in the morning, as every day, against the love-crazed persecutions of the coeds of all grades, who, she claimed, were all whores, as she had excellent reason to know, although she wasn't threatened in the least because Director Voráček in the years with her and owing to her security precautions had added to his mere hundred and thirty pounds another

seventy, and less sightly ones at that, so all students without exception at the Pedagogical Institute referred to him as "Plumpudding," "Walking Bulldozer," or "Zvoráček," that is, "Greaseball," in fact, they used to say when they met him and his lady out walking

"Hey, look at the prexy lurching along with his old bag . . ."

what a gross punishment for the tasteless nicknames he used to heap in summer camp upon his clumsier fellow students, how could one then fail to

understand what that moment of a spring dawn meant to him, when mysterious relays in his brain fused and he put on paper the two commissioned monologues and knew they were

right, they clicked, they were perfect, made to order, parts cut to exact size. It came to him that but for his laziness and cockiness which had impelled him to ring his teacher's doorbell to tell her she might examine him in Czech, she overpowered him, still in the hall, then refused his request anyway, saying literally:

"What about the other boys who got nothing from me . . ."

he was a notorious Don Juan, but the other fellows were apparently wiser—that if it had not been for all that, his scenarios would not be read today by a senile dotard or a raving maniac, but by artists of the first order, yet it was too

late, and that is why when Juráček's, Voráček's, Hábl's and Hudec's paths crossed beneath the disgustingly obese, naked creature surrounded by tall flowers, there were dark rings under their eyes and they were pale as though all four had undergone the identical operation. After Head Resident Hudec had made sure there was nothing serious to the alarm and that from a medical point of view the patient was fully able to carry out publicly his moral duty, he let him shower and get dressed while Comrade Hábl ordered a substantial breakfast which, they unanimously agreed, they could not partake in, not one tiny bite, each one was weighed down by

something that filled him like concrete in the guts before an X-ray treatment, one faced his first public appearance in the role of town and district father, in line, perhaps, for more vital instances of fatherhood if he managed new marriage alliances smartly, the second faced the premiere of his first artistic composition, the third a shameful self-abasement, and the fourth a pointlessly dishevelled and entirely empty

bed which could hardly be repopulated on a Sunday morning since one must remember the door was smashed in. They were sitting in front of the cold eggs, two of them excited, two apathetic, they stared out of the window upon the square bathed in early morning spring light, across which would soon hurry those to take part in the meeting, instead there was the crack of a sudden

thunderclap announcing the first storm of the season, not in human memory had there been one this early, and it was being bruited about that it was God's punishment for dispersing the preceding day the devout women from the restaurant "Filípek," be that as it may, a heavenly bathtub of water was literally upended over K., for a few minutes it seemed as though the entire works had

dropped into water, Comrade Hábl panicked, he came close to letting himself be driven to the dental clinic when he recalled that Comrade Nohýnek had made that trip and that the golden age of dentists was past anyway, because, after all, the decision was his, no one else would do it for him, nor let him off, and he had to decide all on his own, in lofty loneliness, the Minister of Tourism having left at seven with the manager of the Grand Hotel, these boars could have waited, he silently complained to himself, they wouldn't have run away, the receiver was in his hand before he knew it, and he was going to have the local radio station announce that he was postponing Sunday by a day, consequently today was a working day and therefore participation in the meeting would be

obligatory for the invited student body and workers' representatives, but he couldn't get a signal for a very long time since during the night he had personally yanked out the wires, by the time he remembered, there was no further need of calling, because all four caught sight of a mass of naked

bodies approaching through the solid wall of water. At first they thought the intrusive naked boy in the picture had remained stuck to their retinas, but it promptly became clear that the citizens had simply made the discovery that the downpour had reached an intensity against which umbrellas and raincoats, even those of foreign make, offered no protection, and therefore, since the morning was warm, had done the most logical thing they could, namely, to undress to their

bathing suits, so that they were in fact swimming through town and having arrived at the Grand Hotel rented

bath towels at the usual rates. When half an hour later Comrade Hábl with his covey ascended the podium, passing along the pipes of the giant organ, one was reminded by this ballroom, this elegant *Jugendstil* showboat, equipped with crystal chandeliers, marble stairways and columns, shell-shaped balconies and a painted skylight, more of the

Roman senate, it must be said that the prospect offered by a thousand people dressed in nothing but their bath towels which concealed all differences in age, sex, social status, and cast of mind, that this prospect, elsewhere certain to shock, was nothing unusual for K., since all the townspeople more or

less made their living from the operations of the resort. They being overheated, first from the wild race though the rain, then from rubbing themselves dry and finally from crowding on the floor and in the balconies, a faint steam hung in the ballroom so that Comrade Hábl had the feeling he had come into a fair-sized

sauna, they were received with applause and whistles, an incontrovertible proof that opinions were divided, but Comrade Hábl, an experienced official, knew that applause and whistles were the work of microscopic extremist groups, while in the middle like a big, plump, yet still useful and reliable animal reposed the indifferent masses and to

fight for them was what it was all about. He gave a sign and the loudspeakers subsided, the one to the left of the hall had played woodwind music, the one to the right, jazz, an arrangement he had prescribed in order to underscore from the very beginning that he deemed it his function to rise above generational conflicts, now he rose as the silence took hold and without prefatory remarks or introducing anyone began to read his address, on the one hand he was afraid that on mentioning the name Adam Juráček it might come to a

demonstration, on the other, he wanted to show how in contrast to Kreperát, who loved pomp, and to Mareš, who liked to hear himself make pithy speeches, he was going to speak the way he was going to act, sober, terse, to the point, in that sense he carried out Minister Nauman's charge to Voráček. The latter had

accomplished it, indeed, he had done more than had been asked of him, in the morning, seized by an orgasmic creative upsurge, he had written for Comrade Hábl a most faithfully typecast speech, which the latter had failed to look over ahead of time, and he discovered, he

soon discovered, he soon discovered in dismay, that he, discovered in dismay, that also in the written, discovered in dismay, that also in the written speech the words, soon discovered that also in the written speech he had to, discovered in dismay, that in the written speech he had to repeat words, dismay, repeat words as when he talked

extemporaneously, he reddened in anger, which fortunately was not noticed in the steaming ballroom and promised himself that right after the meeting he'd have Director Voráček transferred, transferred to the furthermost border of the district to a Fresh-Air

School,* but at the moment he was helplessly at the mercy of the text, obediently he repeated and repeated and repeated, aware of how the impact of the case faded, together with his authority, therefore he put more expression into the words, his voice assumed a cutting undertone, he spoke as though he were hacking the words

with a sword from the page, in these minutes and before everyone's eyes his personality changed, and those present had no problem realizing that a man was talking to them whom they had never known, that they were dealing with

a new Comrade Hábl who would boss them more severely than Comrade Kreperát, not to mention Comrade Mareš, the silly text won a new resonance in his mouth and fell like a triphammer upon the head

of Adam Juráček, who only now grasped the full import of his situation, he saw that he was well launched on a downhill slide to forfeit, beyond the little platform with the siding that reminded one of a toy train, beyond his marvellous gift, beyond Kateřina Horová, his beloved

profession. He caught sight of his mother sitting in the first row, it was impossible to miss her, surrounded by so many people naked but for their bathing suits, for with the rising temperature the towel-togas had come off one by one, there she sat, she and an old man next to her, dressed in ceremonial

black such as is customary at village funerals. Although he had never seen him, he guessed he was his uncle and his mother's brother, František Hopner, who had come here in order to be a support to his sister in this difficult hour and thus perhaps make up a little for the loss of the

*These are school buildings established in the mountains or woods, where students from other parts of the country, especially the larger cities, take monthly turns at some fresh air.

cuckoo-clock which at one time he had withheld from her although she loved it beyond anything, he couldn't bear their looking at him, these two old people broken by such disgrace in the evening of their lives, a disgrace caused, moreover, by their own flesh and blood, he tore his glance from them and with unsteady hands hidden under the table turned the first page of the text

Director Voráček had prepared for him, to find out to what depth his humiliation must sink and whether there was even one oyster-pearl's worth of hope with which he might propel himself to the surface. He was relieved to discover that the text surprisingly enough mirrored his intellectual level and manner of expression rather accurately, he sounded reserved, modest, and, presented in short

yet not choppy sentences, neither pigheaded nor self-demeaning, he did not make him sprinkle

dung upon his own head. In the speech he was to state openly, without losing himself in details which could at best create but new confusions, that he had indeed been occupied with the by now well-known project, of course purely in theory, but since he noted that it not only contradicted the law of gravity of the great Newton, whom he had loved, honored, and obeyed since childhood, but that it also, and beyond it, was being misused in the dissemination of flimsy

myths, which threatened law and order of the town as well as the peaceful pursuit of work by honest citizens and above all interfered with the fruitful education of our youth—as a citizen and, more important, as a

teacher he had no choice but to pull the rug from under such rumors once and for all and at the same time declare he would desist from any further experimentation in this field, while he longed, could they summon that much confidence in him, to make up for his mistake by redoubling his work in the drawing class and

gym of the Pedagogical Institute in K., for which purpose he asked them to take into consideration his totally irreproachable past thrown into shadow only in the last few days when in his despair he sought recourse in al

cohol and had indeed incurred certain debts which he was going to pay off in instalments by part-time work Saturdays and Sundays in the construction of the monument to the great Newton. He could hardly finish reading without holding back his tears, and he fumbled under the table for the hand of his Director and friend

Voráček to thank him that for the second time in his life he had been ready to leap to his assistance, but he could not catch hold of it because a little earlier all hands in the ballroom had been raised in applause following the address of Comrade Hábl whose remorseless, implacable tone alarmed many in the audience to such a degree that they not only let him hear but also

see how unconditionally they agreed with him. Comrade Hábl sat down, accepting the congratulations of Director Voráček, who was ecstatically elated that his art had found in Comrade Hábl a better interpreter than he could have suspected, while Comrade Hábl hissed icily to the author to report to his office at twelve sharp, and commanded his other neighbor, this wretch on his right, to up and do his moral duty. So Adam Juráček

rose enveloped by a hot, moist silence, a silence in which hung suspended disappointment on the right and vindictive satisfaction on the left, he once again unfolded his speech when, before he could even speak the first word, he felt

unwell, he had to shut his eyes for an instant, he rallied all the forces within him, breathed in deeply, breathed out, and joyfully discovered that it was over, that he was once again

fit, he believed he would succeed in winning their renewed confidence and at the same time reconquer for good his place on firm ground, nearly lost because of his pride, the ground upon which Kateřina Horová lived, surely she must be waiting for him, and he would deliver his speech, throw off the incubus, and run to her over that same firm ground so that until their blissful end they would glow in each other's happiness upon the

ground, he opened his eyes and mouth in order to start, but to his amazement he saw his audience, he saw Comrade Hábl, he saw the entire ballroom

upside down, because he stood high above the table of the chairman on the painted skylight, below him the subsiding pitter-patter of the rain, above him a thousand bewildered, flabbergasted faces in the balconies and still higher, way up high on the floor of the ballroom, but the worst thing of all was that not a one of them made the least sound, at first he wanted to fall

upwards in the simpleminded hope of talking his way out of it, but although he pushed himself off as vigorously as he could, he landed again on the glass surface of the skylight beneath which the sun had appeared this very moment, the first

uproar broke out, the entire ballroom was filled with ear-splitting applause and whistles, the left side whistled, the right applauded, while those susceptible to giddiness fainted or escaped into the corridors, then

two shots were fired, he saw policemen wrestling with Comrade Hábl at the chairman's table, he was brandishing someone's service revolver and wanted to

shoot him down, but he'd been in the army before the war and at that in the Quartermaster Corps, he merely hit the upper register of the organ, which began to emit a sound like a siren, it was this which woke up Adam Juráček, now he knew that

he had conquered, that after the

crisis, which he had experienced in the shoe store and which had reached its peak in the toilet of the train station, he had regained his

lost potency

completely, without

becoming conscious of it, he reacted like a frustrated prisoner who after years of deprivation in jail meets up with a hot girl friend, and he began, as before in the depressing

urinal, to jump around like a maniac, this time however not from desperation, but in pure, utterly unadulterated

joy, he waved to his students who, directed by Václav Klokoč, cheered him a thunderous hip-hip-hooray, he threw kisses to his mother whom he saw once again cry in happiness, sitting next to her black-coated brother František Hopner who managed to be the only one to keep his composure, for as a villager he was naturally distrustful, he was used to judge the harvest only after it was stowed in the

barn. He danced and sang to the accompaniment of the screaming organ pipes and screaming women until he became weary, then lay down, pleasantly exhausted, upon the

ballroom ceiling, a dark shadow against the gleaming rainbow visible through the skylight, and in the meantime above his head continued the roiling

hell.

LEAFLET 1

distributed during the student demonstration on Main Street in the morning of March 21, 19--.

(The text is handwritten.)

Fathers!

Wake up! You've been sleeping too long! In your sleep you've preached us lies!

You taught us that man is master of creation, but you have wasted your lives in the jail of dogmas!

That wasn't enough for you! You wanted to lock us up too, your sons and grandsons!

You've papered the jail with washing machines, refrigerators and cars so that truth about the world doesn't get to us!

You mobilized against the truth bureaucrats, scientists, journalists and the clergy, all as far gone in age as you!

This morning you were still trying to tell us the greatest discovery in the history of man was a fraud!

But the revolution marching forward in South America, Asia, and Africa is not going to be stopped by a barricade of lies, not even before the gates of K.!

Your preposterous resolutions, erratic like today's weather, won't change one iota the fact that human intellect has conquered the primitivism of gravity!

We despise you, but that doesn't mean that we don't love our town K., our country, and all of progressive mankind!

Because we are for these, we are against you, against your stupidity, your rigidity, your hypocrisy, your cowardice!

You are of the same mold as those who burned Jan Hus and violently forced Galileo to recant!

We don't acknowledge your power! But because you have to keep feeding us we are dispensing with violence for the time being!

We shall simply boycott you, we shall boycott your press, your radio, your movies, your theater, your shops, and especially your schools!

We are going to live in communes! We shall jointly throw off gravity so we can look at you as you deserve—down from above!

Down with your paper tiger Newton!

Up with Adam Juráček!

> The Revolutionary Students and
> Apprentices of K.
> 3/21/19--
> (Mankind's First Day of Spring)

LEAFLET 2

distributed during the march of older townspeople of K. in the afternoon of March 21, 19--.

(The text is mimeographed.)

Citizens!

We have been trying to jolt you out of your blunted sense of responsibility for a long time. We have struggled against it at every opportunity, protested, and raised the question by whom, how, where, why, for what reason, and for what purpose our young people are being led.

We have consecrated our whole life to the struggle against the dregs of the dark past. We have been beaten neither by terror, war, hunger, misery, nor by plagues, frosts, heat waves, floods, and other disasters. We have concluded the struggle in victory because we were heartened by the knowledge that after the end of the struggle in our old age we could look forward to the gratitude and esteem of our children.

How immense our surprise, however, when instead of gratitude and esteem, the bitterest disappointment awaited us. The seeds of a new conflict have been sown between us and our children, all the more terrible because it takes place under the auspices of the very power we struggled for.

The purpose of our struggle was to pass on the fruits of it directly to our sons and daughters. It turned out, however, that this job was entrusted to the rottenest intellectuals who weren't in the least embarrassed to hide behind the cloak of educators.

We too went to school way back and will always remember our favorite teachers, men and women, with genuine love. Their struggle was to teach us to read and write, to multiply and divide as well as possible. We rated this so high that we did not hesitate to attend school even if we had to hike a long way, if need be barefoot.

We are not against education. Have we not struggled that the most recent generation should learn more than we did and that they should be able to ride to school by the most modern means of transportation without a struggle and in decent shoes?

Surely we did not struggle for those rotten intellectuals referred to to teach our children how to go beyond us. We did not struggle that a struggle-weary father, who struggled untiringly his whole life through, watches at the end of it how his son cynically tramples on the ceiling upon all those things we struggled for.

Citizens!

Struggle against these abuses in a way that was passed from our most loyal, struggling forbears to our fathers and grandfathers.

So-called "modern" methods are all too familiar, and where have they taken us? Let's look in the attics for the old canes, let's cut us switches from willows, let's buy us sticks and rods, let's unbuckle our belts, let's roll up our sleeves in the good old way and give them as good a whipping as we once got!

So they should know what we struggled for!

Alliance of Parents of K.

LEAFLET 3

distributed in K. in the evening of March 21, 19--, by *declassé*
elements and others.

Comrades!
  We call upon you!
All of you who have been forced for decades to walk on the
ceiling!
Don't let yourselves be taken in by the Lilliput war between
the daddies and their boys!
They are from one and the same mold!
Yesterday the daddies kicked our faces in!
Tomorrow their boys will do the same!
Let them quarrel over gravity!
We've been robbed of more than that!
The time has come!
Let's take it back!
Let's show them who we are, what we want!
Paving stones haven't lost their force of gravity!

Fighters for Human Rights of the town K.

[Note: The text of this leaflet is, in contrast to the others,
printed, and, in fact, on slick paper. One may boldly charac-
terize it as a unique graphic work, since it is undated and its
heading a color lithograph of the town K. in prewar days as
evidenced by the signboards of formerly private business
concerns. Some of these facts might raise the suspicion it was
a matter of planned provocation, which the passage of so
many years makes it impossible to substantiate.]

EXECUTIVE ORDER

of March 21, 19--.

In view of the fact that despite several notices and warnings on the part of higher administrative authorities, despite information campaigns by mass media, and despite numerous releases by scientific, clerical, educational, athletic, and other institutions, repeated provocations and disturbances have taken place in the town of K.,

A State of Emergency

is hereby declared by the government according to Par. 307, Sections 2 and 3 of the Code of Criminal Procedure, to be in effect in the town and entire district of K.,

for purposes of prosecuting punishable acts against public safety according to Section 179 of the Code of Criminal Law, which have taken particularly dangerous hold in the town and district of K.

Without regard to sex, age, religion, or other distinctions, all residents are forthwith prohibited from

(a) walking on walls and ceilings of rooms irrespective of whether they are public or private quarters;

(b) raising themselves without the assistance of motors or other mechanical devices (for flying, the assistance of motors and other mechanical devices falls under the provisions and regulations currently in effect);

(c) distributing any and all claims that contest the validity of the so-called law of gravity formulated by I. Newton and reconfirmed at tonight's administrative session on the basis of consultations at home and abroad, in any form whatsoever, whether verbal, or by graffiti, leaflets, or other illegal means of reproduction.

Responsibility for the executing of this part of the Order

rests with the Minister of the Interior, who will dispatch the needed forces to K. in order to ensure and preserve public order.

An air squadron will be stationed in K. to ensure compliance with the above prohibitions.

Responsibility for this rests with the Minister of Defense, who will take measures to prevent any unwelcome shooting down of civil or agricultural aircraft, as well as woodcocks migrating from their nesting places.

In the entire district of K. instruction in physics and mathematics at all grade levels of all types of schools is to cease temporarily.

Responsibility here rests with the Minister of Education, who will implement the reassignment of all faculties.

The instigator(s) who has (have) been the cause of the present situation will be legally prosecuted.

Authority responsible: the Minister of Justice who pledges himself that there will be no infringements of, or encroachments upon, laws now in force.

For purpose of implementing the law concerning the State of Emergency, the government dismisses the present administrative head of K., Jan Hábl, who succeeded neither in preventing the development of the current situation, nor in controlling it, and appoints until further notice Comrade Miloš Nohýnek to this post.

At the same time, the government has accepted the resignation of the Minister of Tourism, Nauman, submitted by the latter after it had been urged upon him by telephone, and has entrusted his department to the Minister of the Interior.

The purport of this order consists by no means in returning to the days of Galileo or even Giordano Bruno whose scientific insights were reliably confirmed by subsequent ages, so that we can unreservedly pass them on to our younger generation, but rather to prevent the perversion of our country's efforts in scientific and technological progress by charlatans and careerists as well as by dubious elements and individuals who would turn the wheel of history back into a dark past. It lies entirely in the hands of the town and district citizens of K. as to when this Order will,be lifted by the government, for its aim is to protect the aspirations of upright citizens in the overwhelming majority of other districts and towns of our country.

Head of Government
(signed)

CODED DISPATCH

from the Federal Government in Berne to the Swiss Embassy in Prague 1, Hradčanské nám. 1, March 21, 19--.

2937	3942	2638	9742	1199	0296	7283	2314
2938	3792	7421	9238	2937	1987	7391	2892
1756	8439	8593	2793	5493	1867	1234	5678
9098	7654	3210	53	6666			

[Note: Innumerable similar dispatches were sent and received by the code clerks of foreign missions in Prague during that eventful spring week. The example above demonstrates the degree of interest with which even the Swiss Federal President inquired into the significance of the events in K. apparently on the basis of a message from Prague diplomats. This is understandable, for Switzerland had preserved her neutrality and independence during the last war owing only to the fact that there existed no effective weapons against this Alpine fortress. Leading European politicians and military experts concurred with domestic politicians and experts. This gave rise to the severest censorship since the end of war being imposed even in Western Europe on all the information received, especially from K. Emergency laws were invoked. Responsible authorities apparently wished to prevent a universal panic as well as a lowering in morale among NATO members. Whatever the reasons, the fact remains that the only allusion at that time appeared in the Swiss publication *Zivilverteidigung* (published by Miles in Aarau) on pp. 145–46, which ran in the first version as follows: "Long before there is any violent conflict, in the midst of peace, the enemy is hard at work . . . to destroy our self-confidence and undermine our powers of resistance. . . . Those who want to ruin us systematically sow doubt and fear. We do not trust them. We are not frightened by so-called scientific theories that predict the fall of countries and cultures or even *gravitation* [later version: the world]. We are alert. We are fortunate to have experienced *weight* [later version: peace]. . . . We are not *lighter* [later version: weaker] than other nations and our forefathers." The printing of the edition with the first version was interrupted and the run-off copies were officially reduced to pulp, except for two, which were accidentally sent to a Czech writer in place of the author's copies of his latest book. Today those copies are naturally worth their weight in gold. No one is surprised that up to now the writer has refused to sell them although the Swiss government has made an offer for them of free asylum for ten individuals and work permits for two. The first uncensored mention of the case appears in the posthumously published diary of the English King Charles III, the son of the last British Queen Elizabeth. The entire entry is worth quoting: "Sunday, March 21, 19--, brought us an item of news from Prague, which the Prime Minister in person and by helicopter delivered to us in Scotland. It brought our game with Prince Philip, Duke of Edinburgh and our father, to a close, thank God. We were thereby saved certain defeat, though at what price? After all the calamities, can our empire really be spared nothing? Are we faced with another Battle of Britain? God save the King! By the way, could one play golf on the ceiling?" The above-mentioned dispatch from the Federal Government in Berne to its representative in Prague is remarkable for another reason, namely, that its message remained incomprehensible even after successful decipherment. Experts suspected it was a matter of a "double-code," but a handpicked team failed to identify the key. Since the job nevertheless had to be done, it was tentatively concluded that a technical malfunction had garbled the message. Only when fifteen years later the gifted young counter-intelligence student Jáno Malatínský was looking through the Archive of Curiosities, did he discover that the Bernese code clerk, clearly in a state of excitement, based the encipherment on his first language, Schwytzer-dütsch, which is today still spoken by the inhabitants of the German-speaking areas of Switzerland, especially in cantons Uri, Schwyz, and Unterwalden, and of course Lucerne.]

WARRANT OF ARREST

executed by the District Attorney of K. on March 21, 19--.

The District Attorney of K. orders the immediate arrest of JURÁČEK, Adam, born 12/24/19--, in K., lately residing in K., 1 Park Street, last employed as Professor of Physical Education and Drawing at the Pedagogical Institute in K., in compliance with Par. 68 of the Code of Criminal Procedure and the State of Emergency imposed by the government on the town and district of K. on March 21, 19--.

At the same time, a search is to be made of aforementioned individual's living quarters as well as of his place of work, including the art studio and gymnasium, with special attention to be given to leaflets, printed matter and other objectionable literature of anti-gravitational content. Any objectionable material discovered together with the individual mentioned are to be delivered to the District Attorney in K.

Issued in K., March 21, 19--, at 11:15 p.m.

Signed (in his own hand):
Bedřich Řeřicha, Major (Reserves)
District Attorney in K.

Epilogue

RECONSTRUCTION 9

(According to contemporary records)

When they led him
from his house, the street resembled an arena despite the
late hour, no one was allowed on the street according to the
imposed State of Emergency but nothing had been said about
windows, they were open and crowded like theater
boxes, when they entered the house the policemen were
greeted by frenetic clapping from the older and ear-splitting
whistles by the younger inhabitants of K., now as the prisoner came into view, the opposing parties swapped reactions,
youth applauded, and age
hooted. They looked forward to seeing a pale, dishevelled,
perhaps weeping derelict, at least one crushed by the weight
of fear and
handcuffs. Frankly, that's how he had seen himself a moment ago when the intoxication of triumph had fled, which
he had enjoyed beneath the witches' cauldron of the topsy-
turvy ballroom, and when he ran home on the roofs of the
arcades, first because his pleasure had not subsided and se-
condly to escape the ovations and the volleys of spit, he

observed the coming into being of the first

demonstration. He watched with amazement how his students, whom he knew from his drawing class and gym as the spineless sons of former revolutionaries and whom he would not have believed capable of committing themselves

to anything, how these boys who measured the world by rock-decibels, and the girls who, when asked last year to illustrate their favorite book, had brought him extremely realistic drawings for the *Kamasutra* of Vatsyayana, it made him

sick for a week, how

this strange social entity of colorless, spoilt, and selfish individuals, forcibly and accidentally driven together by the law of compulsory education, all of a sudden united in doctrinal action and within a few minutes turned into a

generation, he was genuinely

frightened, he realized for the first time that he was fully responsible for it, he and no one else, it could hardly be denied that the spark which ignited the hidden dynamite charge of enthusiasm and rejection was his

doing, he realized that as teacher he should have approached them and done that which he had not done in the ballroom, namely, to pull the manuscript from his pocket and read them the speech which Director Voráček had composed and by exploiting the

unquestionable loyalty he had won from them find a way to calm them, to convince them that they were too

young to arrive at long-range decisions on the basis of superficial

impressions, to urge them to go home peacefully and eat their Sunday dinner lovingly prepared by their mothers, and to continue to honor their fathers and teachers who only wanted what was

best for them, it was his duty, and he knew it, he came to a decision, his fear melted away, he believed again that a single step by him would pour oil on troubled waters, the

second step, bar the way to the masses, the third, cool overheated heads, and the fourth, turn the course of events
against the tide, back to that place where

the mistake had occurred, it remained a pious hope, however, of all the planned steps he did not even take the first,
he was still the prisoner of his newly sprouted

potency, he was her

plaything, however vigorously he pushed himself off he
always returned from the lowest depths back to the ceiling,
at last it became clear to him that he was likely to smash his
head against the marble walk of the arcade, or, worse, that
the students would interpret it as another ploy for

approbation, like a swarm of bees, fear attacked him again,
he took to flight, he fled from vault to vault of the arcades
at the time fortunately devoid of people, crossed the river on
the underside of the bridge's arch and came to rest only on
the *Jugendstil* stucco of the hall at 1

Park Street, fear took hold of him and drowned out the
state of subdued gravity, at least to the degree that he succeeded after a few attempts to lower himself to his door, to
ring the bell, but no one

was at home, he unlocked, dragged himself to his room
and threw himself upon his bed, pressed his eyes shut, and
longed for sleep, to sleep everything away, but sleep wouldn't
come, he rose to look for Isonal, Dormidel, or Hexobarbital,
or even Pentobarbital, at least Valium, he merely found

Nightal, for which he was

grateful, but hardly had he put it in his mouth than he
began to choke, his stomach convulsed in the

rhythm of the Head Resident's pump, it dawned on him
that the compassion afforded by barbiturates and sedatives
would be denied him the rest of his life, that from this day
forward he would have to

face in full consciousness the pains of his body and soul,
fear overran him like water a stalagmite, oppressed and
crushed his body, he lay limp on his bed, stripped to his

125

nerves. It was absurd. Why, he asked himself in despair, since no one else was near except God perhaps, but he had never believed in him, why had this prostration not occurred an hour earlier in the ballroom when it would have made sense, when it would have put things to rights, why has it happened now when I should be packing my bare necessities and be off, flee

as far as my feet will carry me from this town run amok, whose streets resound with roars from youthful throats and then are drowned out by others coated with gallons of

beer, he recalled the battles of last century which shifted between two commanding summits over a few declivities, fields, valleys, and mountain tops, how happily he would have included this battle among all those he had successfully forgotten together with the names of statesmen and generals, but the catch was that the battle was about

him, he heard for a while his name re-echo like a bell in the voices of the clashing parties and then crack like a

nut, this noise drove into his

marrow, and when towards evening it was replaced by the screeches of the *declassé* elements and others, who used his name like a ramrod against bulletin boards, shop windows, and the whole political

system, he knew that he was irrevocably

lost, he no longer had the strength even to cover his ears, he lay helpless on his bed, locked in by his fear like a snail in its house, like a caterpillar in its cocoon, yes, worse, like a pit in a plum, like the carp in

aspic, waiting for the fourth and ultimate noise on which he was counting with absolute certainty, the merciless, uniform footstep of hobnailed boots, he had no idea that modern armies no longer move on

foot, when he heard the rattling of the first caterpillar track, the taut spring of his horror catapulted him from his bed to the

floor, where he remained lying incapable of any movement, then in glowing heat he began to envy his forerunner of long ago, the man from Syracuse to whom it was granted in a like difficult hour to look into the face of his enemy of flesh and blood and to fling at him his

"Noli tangere circulos meos . . ."

true, he was stabbed, but there was a human shape to it, his murderer remembered the expression, made a joke of it, how else would it have found its way into

schoolbooks, he couldn't even imagine what he was going to say once the wall burst, the wall that stood between him and Park Street, and a wholly impersonal armored

monster entered his quiet room. He occupied himself with these tortuous thoughts a long time. After the armored trucks had left the resort section of town and, although they didn't have the required VVIP stickers, were driving along the arcades to the town center, he heard the loudspeaker strangely distanced even though attached to the house (his mother often and secretly plugged it with a

sponge), heard it announce the State of Emergency, and one sentence literally howled into his ear as though someone had turned the volume to maximum:

"Presumed instigators will be prosecuted . . ."

at which point he began to envy another teacher of his, "Show him the instruments . . ."

the teacher who when he caught sight of the instruments of torture was permitted to recant his anti-heliocentric teachings, leave the horror chamber and return to the blue Florentine skies, how much he would have liked to do the same, he was prepared to recant even his own name, suddenly a final

hope flared up, he hugged it as he lay there quite paralyzed as though he were never going to move any part of his body again, not to mention raising himself like a butterfly to the sky and overcome the force of gravity, which even compels a flying projectile to return to earth, he tried to profit by it, tried to

obliterate his gift, and he knew something about that. He

closed his eyes, pressed his teeth together, stopped breathing, and mobilized and concentrated all reserves of will power to wipe away that gift as he had formerly wiped away English, the ability to write, Prakrit languages, and the names of generals and statesmen, so he remained for several long minutes until he ran out of

oxygen, but he didn't let go, he was determined to lose consciousness if necessary, if the onrushing cerebral anemia should destroy the blocked brain cells, he was well on the way, there was a ringing in his ears, he saw red, he felt an infinite release and the premonition that he had attained his end when the

clatter of breaking glass and an almost simultaneous blow on his back startled him, and he

stared, once again flat on the ceiling, eyes ajar, upon the remains of the lighting fixture's frosted globe which he had shattered in his undirected upward flight, no, he could afford no illusions, it was

useless, his gift simply was in him, invisible yet invincible like hot-flowing

magma, it did not let itself be forgotten, not even pumped out with the Head Resident's pump, it had entered his

blood and he had to bear his

lot whatever it might be, unfortunately he knew it, not the least uncertainty was granted him, his lot was precisely predetermined by the paragraph in the Executive Order concerning the legal prosecution of the

instigators, what

use to have been born in an enlightened century where he was threatened neither by a Greek spear nor papal instruments of torture. A man acclimatizes himself, alas, too quickly so that nowadays he grows nervous when he merely pictures an ordinary, common, civilized, regularly disinfected

prison. Lying on the ceiling, he was as paralyzed by this thought as he had earlier been on the floor although it would have meant for him no great change since he had spent the last months in the voluntary solitary confinement of his room, all of a sudden he felt a stab of acute longing for

nature, he recalled his hikes from K. to Prague and back and regretted bitterly that he had passed them absorbed in thoughts, in knitting, or in some other activity, in what a different state of mind he would have done his walking today, he would have paid attention to every flower, every twig of every fir tree, with what abandon he would have stumbled over every bump in the

asphalt, which he had then foolishly wished away because they ruined his shoes, now he saw in them symbols of

freedom. His was a woeful appearance, lying there, the conqueror of gravity, at the stalks of the smashed light, cowering and quivering like a little lap-

dog who had made a puddle, and so literally had he, it glimmered above him on the floor between the broken pieces of glass because for the first time in his life he had

cried, it was a scene for the gods and, even more, a paradisical scene for the absolutely average

examiner, who would certainly have to conclude that a case like this could be taken care of one-

two-three, however when shortly after midnight a police car stopped in front of the house, his mother got out too, supported by her brother František Hopner. Descendants of persecuted Luthcrans, they had a cunning which no one would have credited them with, and they had led the officials to believe that her son was hiding in one of the

organ pipes in the ballroom, it took them three hours until they had cut the last one with an acetylene

torch, the mother trusting he had in the meanwhile fled to the woods, so she was taken to the apartment in a

calm state of mind, he heard the cars and the key, he had all the reason in the world to sink to the bottom of

despair, to collapse into a lamentable bundle of nerves that could have been crammed into a briefcase, but instead

he felt to his amazement his quivering limbs relax, his pulse steady, his mind clear, and the harness of his fear drop from him like

an icicle from the gutter, it was one of those inexplicable reactions that have such unusual results, such as a coward running into a burning house to rescue his neighbor's record player, or a non-swimmer saving a

policeman drowning in a frozen river, a reaction by which ordinary mortals rise to

heroism. He was suddenly

himself again, able to master body and soul, and he proved it to himself that instant by lowering himself effortlessly to the

carpet, even succeeded in kicking the broken pieces of glass swiftly under the bed. When they came into the room, they found him just as they had thought they would find him, self-assured, robust, calm, even smiling, in short, a dangerous

opponent in every respect, ready to

defend his

truth to the very end, to maintain it, preserve it and to protect it, and thus he naturally earned

their respect, they permitted him to take leave of his crying mother and contrary to orders did not even

handcuff him after he had given them his word he wouldn't

float off on the way to the car, he begged Uncle František Hopner to provide his mother shelter under the parental roof for as long as needed and to replace by his care not only the son but also the

cuckoo-clock, which she loved beyond anything, and ignoring everyone, unbroken, almost proud, he walked ahead of the others into the street, which despite the hour resembled a stadium, he marched through a path of applause and whistles, accolade and abuse, to a police car in which he took his seat with as much dignity as though the driver had asked him where

he wanted to go, and he left

1 Park Street, not suspecting that it was

forever, while the older inhabitants converted the younger generation to the true faith with a barrage of

slaps.

EXPERT OPINION

submitted by Assistant Professor Dr. Placenta on May 15, 19--.

In a letter of April 1, 19--, the Municipal Criminal Court of Prague turned to me as a specialist in general physics with the request to offer my expert opinion in Case No. 868–12/19/19--, pending in the above Court. I was asked to

(a) investigate whether Accused XY (I was not given his name) was, by common definition, only partially or not at all subject to the usual force of gravity (that is to say, that his body at such periods is in a state in many terminologies described as "levitational");

(b) explain the nature of this phenomenon.

The case gave rise to a correspondence between myself and the Court, in the course of which I at first rejected the request as a disparagement of myself on the assumption that it constituted a poor joke, to judge by the date of the letter. After I was assured that the case was not only serious but of national importance, and since no obstacles prevailed for purposes of Article 36/19--, of the Code pertaining to experts and interpreters, I have accepted the above assignment.

Preliminary Investigation

On consultation with examining authorities, I visited above-mentioned Accused XY in cell No. 149 in New Prison on April 4, 19--, where in the presence of Vilém Beran, investigator, Pál'o Růžička, guard, and Dr. Ervín Sloup, prison doctor, I explained to Accused the purport of the investigation which was to be undertaken by me in consonance with the above-mentioned decision, and I solicited his personal consent. Accused XY gave it readily and signed a declaration prepared by the doctor in which he confirms that no responsibility will accrue to me, as expert, should there be any impairment of his health.

At 2:11 p.m. I requested Accused XY, in order to prepare minor experiments, to demonstrate the phenomenon that I was to examine in due course. Accused XY concurred and before the eyes of all those present slowly floated upwards, and in such a manner that his back first touched the ceiling, then he slowly rotated until his head was substantially lower than the rest of his body and his feet pressed firmly against the ceiling (height 2331 millimeters). His head was finally approximately 600 millimeters above the floor. In this position he took several steps of average length, which left distinct marks upon the dusty surface of the white ceiling; on further request he changed his position by means of the above-mentioned process, keeping himself upside down, to one common among normal people, that is, crouching upon a bench.

The protocol of this preliminary experiment, signed not only by those mentioned above but by myself too, I submit as Enclosure I.

When it became clear to me that I was dealing with an

unusually demanding assignment I insisted, within the provisions of the mentioned law, on exercising the option of calling in further specialists, in the first place, my teacher, friend, and present Dean of the Natural Science Faculty, Professor Emerich Durych. Furthermore I mentioned the possible size of the fee, which would probably exceed the customary amount. Both of these requests were granted.

Experiment Proper

The preliminary investigation also brought home to me the fact that cell No. 149 was wholly unsuited to a thorough observation of the processes and of the essential nature of the above-mentioned phenomenon, because its low height precluded the installation of complicated experimental equipment. By courtesy of the prison authorities the use of cell No. 120 (measuring 6 x 6 x 4 meters) was made available to me, a cell designed to accommodate up to 120 individuals following planned spontaneous demonstrations and therefore could be described as suitable for the above-mentioned scientific purposes.

In order to rule out interference by third parties or outside factors the experiment was conducted as follows: the experimental apparatus was handled by remote control from another room, the proceedings were filmed by a 16-millimeter camera (kindly put at our disposal by Cartoon Craft Films), the entire scene was observed by a television camera of the Marconi type (kindly put at our disposal by the department store "White Swan"), and Accused was given all instructions via microphone and loudspeaker (put at our disposal, for reasons of economy, by myself). The committee of experts, whose members are mentioned below, was accommodated at the same time in the above-mentioned, temporarily unoccupied, cell No. 149, which is located at an approximate distance of 290 centimeters from cell No. 120, and where all instructions without exception were recorded by an 8-track air-traffic-control tape recorder (kindly put at our disposal by the rock band "Cruel Rabbits").

An objective reading of Accused's body movements was obtained by means of numerous contact wires, which were stretched in a tight net in cell No. 120, connected to a data recording device, made by Honeywell (kindly put at our disposal by the Central Power Station of Prague). The original tapes are attached to this report, Enclosure 2.

The readings reveal that within approximately three seconds in regular intervals the contacts of wires Nos. 8, 78, 178, 278, 378, 478, 578, 678, 778, 878, 978, and 979 were broken, which corresponds to the above-described first phase of the upward floating of Accused's body. Thus it was reliably proved that the body of the Accused, that is, his essential parts, were after the above-mentioned lapse of time at a height of 2279 millimeters above the floor of the cell. (I feel compelled to confess that I did not succeed in accounting properly for the contact break of wire No. 979, which I shall however do if called upon.) In the view of all those present, the upward floating occurred with a certain air of ease (according to Examiner Vilém Beran "with majesticalness"), not dissimilar to the rise of space rockets, types Vostok and Saturn.

In order to prove that Accused XY could overcome earth's gravity not only at will but even without the assistance of mechanical or other means, we moved to a further stage in the experiments. Here Accused was deprived of all articles of clothing in order to preclude the possibility of floating upwards by means of concealed attachments (i.e., floating devices, montgolfieric and inflatable things of all kinds). At the request of the female secretary of the committee a loin-cloth was found for Accused, which upon due examination was sealed.

In the next experimental phase resiliency meters were attached in a certain pattern to the body of Accused with the aid of bandages, meters which were developed by myself for this purpose (for a better understanding, I should explain that this is a device resembling the so-called beam balance which formerly, in times of so-called private enterprise, was used to weigh so-called goods). The readings from these resiliency meters were also televised to cell No. 149 and movements of the naked Accused body were observed via monitor.

From values registered by the resiliency meters (see Enclosure 3) it clearly emerges that the body of Accused, in the period from 10:10.02 to 10:10.58 exerted a continuous, well-articulated gravitational pull, the maximum of which exceeded the body weight of Accused only slightly, who had been weighed before the start of the experiment, after urinating, on a scale made by Berkeley Company (kindly put at our disposal by the Prague Slaughterhouse). Thus it was proved that according to presently valid physical concepts Accused formed a field of force lasting fifty-six seconds, a field whose magnitude was sufficient to counteract the effects of the magnetic field of the above-mentioned nearly naked body.

On the basis of these experiments it can be regarded as irrefutably proven that Accused is capable of overcoming the effects of the magnetic field of the earth upon his temporal frame, and in view of the fact that the above-mentioned experiments were repeated on April 14, 16, 18, 20, 22, and 24, with identical results, it may be assumed that he is able to do it at will. The attending above-mentioned Dr. Ervín Sloup could find no impairment of his physical condition.

Following a week's interval, which I needed for the interpretation of the data obtained, I began on May 5, to carry out the third part of the series of experiments, with the object of determining the dynamics of the phenomenon which Accused XY had demonstrated. I did so by a method which I developed myself and the publication rights of which I herewith reserve.

A special harness designed by me for the purpose was put

on Accused's body. This harness (kindly supplied by the Orthopedia Cooperative) was connected by a special cable to an apparatus which is equipped to exert a variable, yet arbitrarily adjustable pull in the range of 0–550 kilograms. This equipment operated by an automatically programmed unit, controlled by a portable computer of the type PDP 8, made by Digital Computers, Inc. (kindly put at our disposal by the Prague pastry cooks). (My particular thanks for the coding of the program are owing to Dr. Šašinka.)

The purpose of this experimental phase was to determine the reaction rate (changes in the magnetic field produced by Accused XY) in response to external impulses, according to the valid theory on feedback of systems, and to throw light, on analysis of time constants, upon the physical background of the above-mentioned phenomenon in question.

At 8:01.12, by preceding arrangement, Accused was given a visual and aural signal to begin the process of floating upwards, at which point—in contrast to earlier experiments—the body in question was exposed after two seconds and by means of the above-mentioned apparatus to an imposed pull. From the data obtained (Enclosure 4) it appears that Accused compensated practically on the instant for variation in pull, that is, within limits of experimental error. The unequivocal conclusion to be drawn from this is that the feedback, which directs the upward floating, comprises very small time constants, and that chiefly explains why Accused never wobbled when floating upwards.

It is, however, regrettable that the cable (provided with uncommon kindness by the execution squad) broke at a pull of 478 kilograms as a result of hidden faults, so that this experiment was at that point terminated prematurely. At the same time, this fact proved the extraordinary dynamics of the upward floating which evidently responds to external impulses with unimaginable speed. For under different conditions (i.e., at a delayed reaction rate), the above-mentioned body would, upon reduction of the pull, literally smack into the ceiling of cell No. 120 like an insect hitting the windshield of a vehicle moving at high speed. At such moments Accused failed to show the least signs of tension. The only response that can be extracted from the transcript of the 8-track tape recorder is his expression of pleasure couched in a literary phrase when a part of the experimental installation, viz., the harness designed by me, had ceased to pinch his back.

Conclusions

Upon evaluation of the numerical data of all phases of the experiment, recorded throughout on perforated tape and processed by computer IBM 707 made by IBM (rented at my own cost), I feel justified in presenting the following conclusions in response to questions listed in the beginning:

to (a): Subject XY is capable, basically at any time and, according to all appearance, at unlimited time intervals, of overcoming the force of attraction of the earth's gravitational field. The dynamics of the upward floating of his body exceeds in its speed and its ability to react to external impulses all hitherto familiar apparatuses and/or processes. A possibly fraudulent maneuver, common among so-called levitating mediums, I regard in view of the extensive precautionary measures taken as entirely out of the question.

to (b) the actual nature of the above-mentioned mastering of gravity could not be explained, not even by the above-mentioned experiments.

The assertion of the above Subject, that he achieves his results by the exercise of will power and that he might perhaps be able to pass this capacity on to other individuals, falls outside my field of competence, and I recommend that a team of parapsychologists may be entrusted with that investigation. Examiner Vilém Beran has evinced an interest in such a course of study.

The protocol for the set of experiments (see Enclosure 5) was signed by all members of the committee, which was put together by myself for this purpose, that is, by me, by Jakub Kubala, technician at the Institute of Physics at Charles University, by Dr. Ervín Sloup, by Vilém Beran, examiner, by Pal'o Růžička (later Kwame Nkrumah, Jr.), guard, and by the secretary Uli Kalidová, but not by committee member Professor Emerich Durych, who reserved the right to present a dissenting opinion of which I know nothing.

Qualification Certification

I have compiled this report as expert in the field of general physics, appointed by decree of the Minister of Justice in the field of general physics. I have submitted a complete statement of expenses incurred in connection with the above-mentioned report (see Enclosure 6).

> Dr. Kastor Placenta, Assistant Professor, Ph.D.,
> Faculty of Natural Science,
> Charles University,
> domiciled at Prague 10, V Strži 11

May 15, 19--

DISSENTING OPINION

by Professor Emerich Durych to the Expert Opinion of Assistant Professor Placenta of May 15, 19--.

For thirty-eight years I have had the honor to bestow upon the students of the Faculty of Natural Science of time-honored Charles University my disinterested scientific and scientific-administrative expertise, and, as it happens, at the most varied academic levels, from the post of humble demonstrator, to underpaid assistant, later as assistant professor, then as full professor and even as Dean, to which position I was appointed on March 21 of this year in order to make my contribution in this unusually demanding and indisputably not easy period by means of my rich experience and proven prudence to a renewed strengthening of values temporarily showing signs of faltering.

It suffices to turn the pages of the book of those thirty-eight years in order not only to recreate in the memory of our contemporaries the tortuous path which progressive physics had to traverse before she could achieve her present triumphant success, as for instance represented by peace missions of atomic submarines, but also to recreate just as graphically the irrefutable and undeniable fact that I was honored to be a direct and personal contemporary of Planck, Einstein, Bohr, Schrödinger, Fok, Yukawa, and other outstanding men and thereby offer a not insignificant contribution to the not inconsiderable discoveries in national and international physics of the present day.

I find it impossible to avoid stressing that these and similar brilliant feats of our group are purely and simply owing to the fact that not one of us doubted, not even for one second, indeed depended upon, the incontestably classical work of my predecessor I. Newton, the *Philosophiae Naturalis Principia Mathematica,* a work of crystal purity which incorporates the collective wisdom of all optimally progressive physicists of the world, myself not excluded, and which in conjunction with the results of our own work makes it possible to march forward without obstacles and unburdened by problems.

For these reasons and many others hardly less telling, I can do no other than take fundamental exception to the positivistic-pragmatic Expert Opinion of Assistant Professor Kastor Placenta & company in the case of the supposed upward floating of experimental subject XY, alias Adam

Juráček, which is, not only in my own view, a calculated chess move in a dangerous campaign to cast everything in doubt, everything attained and achieved by us in the last thirty-eight years in progressive physics.

In the name of future generations of physicists, whose very own interest I must protect in the name of the functions conferred upon me without respect of person, I can do no other than exhort Assistant Professor Placenta either to recall his ephemeral-opportunistic Expert Opinion or to remove himself from our Faculty to a place where he can no longer exercise his nihilistic-negativistic influence upon the younger generation at government expense.

[Note: The discovered original of the text is written with a liquid of a peculiarly colorless tint which experts at the Crime Laboratory identify upon chemical analysis as definitely Rh-positive human blood, type B. Searches into old card-index files of the Institute of Public Health reveal that the immortal Professor Emerich Durych belonged to that blood group too. However one judges the content of the above text today, one cannot avoid seeing—to put it reverently in one of Professor Emerich Durych's favorite expressions—that it is the effluence of the author's deepest convictions.]

FROM THE CONFRONTATION

between Professor Emerich Durych and Assistant Professor Kastor Placenta in the presence of Deputy Attorney General, Dr. Libor Bor, on May 25, 19--.

(Transcript of the tape recording)

Dr. Bor: . . . for cutting in, but otherwise we aren't going to get anywhere. You have to understand that your Expert Opinion, for which, as I look at these figures, we have really spared no expense, is to serve as a basis for an indictment which not only according to law must observe a deadline but also, let me put it this way, from an acute social need. Look, let's put our cards on the table. The situation in K.—the news has spread, nothing one can do about that, a district like that is a bag of fleas, one can screw it down tight like a pressure cooker, somebody is still going to spill it among the people, foreign spies, a class enemy, and if not him then at least some cop who wants to make an impression, he brags to his girl friend, so that the situation not only in K. but also outside, let's not kid ourselves, it changes nothing, as long as it doesn't come to a trial, let me stress that, a regular trial, a fair trial, which convinces the people—I repeat: convinces them that they have painted themselves into a corner. We've got to do that, Comrades, by June 21, because that's when summer begins, school vacations, everybody's vacation, and we, that is, the government, can't keep fifty thousand people confined in house arrest, they'd grind the town to pulp— and what happens to the resort business? We've put ourselves in your hands—and you? Two points-of-view are being defended here, which, let me put it this way, cancel each other. I therefore beg you urgently to reply to the following questions responsibly and unequivocally: do each of you stick to your opinion?

Asst. Prof. Placenta:

Yes!

Prof. Durych: Yes!

Dr. Bor: And there is no chance, not a ray, let me put it this way, not a tiny glimmer of hope, that you two can get together?

Prof. Durych: No!

Asst. Prof. Placenta:

No!

Dr. Bor: I don't want to keep it secret from you, Comrades, that the view of Comrade Professor Durych suits me, suits all of us, much better, for one thing, the authority of the deanship stands behind him, for another, don't be mad at me, Comrade Placenta, the case is thereby somehow, how shall I put it, solved. What if we—this is for the time being merely a suggestion—agree to the effect that one of you withdraws his Opinion so that we call upon just one expert, let

	us assume for the sake of argument, the Professor.
Prof. Durych:	True.
Asst. Prof. Placenta:	
	Who?
Dr. Bor:	Professor Emerich Durych.
Asst. Prof. Placenta:	
	Comrade Deputy, while I'm not a dean, I claim the scientist's integrity. The experiments were designed by me, conducted by me, and brought to a conclusion by me.
Dr. Bor:	Does that really matter? When all is said and done, Comrade Professor is your teacher and, you know, your friend.
Both:	Was!
Dr. Bor:	But Comrades!
Prof. Durych:	I hardly believe I can help being ashamed of a student who is not prepared to defend gravity.
Asst. Prof. Placenta:	
	And I must be ashamed of a teacher who rejects scientific proof.
Prof. Durych:	What proof? I ask you, what proof?
Asst. Prof. Placenta:	
	You've seen it in my presence with your own eyes.
Prof. Durych:	I saw nothing.
Dr. Bor:	What's that?
Asst. Prof. Placenta:	
	What do you mean—saw nothing?
Prof. Durych:	I repeat: I saw nothing.
Asst. Prof. Placenta:	
	That's the end!

Dr. Bor:	Wait. Permit me. That changes the situation I'd say quite drastically. Are you prepared, Comrade Professor, to swear to this in court?
Prof. Durych:	I don't know why not.
Asst. Prof. Placenta:	
	For heaven's sake, you would swear that you did not see what I saw, the examiner saw, the guard saw, the technician saw, Miss Kalidová saw and who knows who else?
Professor Durych:	I don't know why not.
Asst. Prof. Placenta:	
	Then I am indeed sorry it has come to this point, but I have to say to you: you are a liar!
Dr. Bor:	But Comrades!
Professor Durych:	I am merely a physicist, my dear colleague, of the good old school, which maintained its preference for precise calculations rather than superficial impression and pious hope. If the man was under the delusion that he walked on the ceiling and you were willing to observe that, well, that is your and his purely private affair. My lifelong scientific experience and my calculations absolutely preclude such an event and confirm conclusively the validity of the present laws. I am indebted to that law insofar as, in contrast to you, I have never seen anyone on the ceiling and never shall.
Dr. Bor:	I think I have to translate this to the appropriate authorities, because I really

see in it, let me put it this way, a way out.

Asst. Prof. Placenta:

Then you can kiss a regular trial goodbye, because you're going to have to find a blind presiding judge.

[Note: In the trial of AJ neither Professor Emerich Durych nor Assistant Professor Placenta gave evidence, because the former was immediately appointed delegate, while proceedings were initiated against the latter on account of punishable findings of dereliction in handling funds and valuable objects. See below.]

ENCLOSURE 6

of the Expert Opinion of Assistant Professor Placenta.

Cost of Equipment and Materials (see receipts):

2–16-millimeter cameras by kind arrangement	Kčs 8,000.00
1–Marconi television camera by kind arrangement	13,250.00
1–Honeywell Data Recording Device by kind arrangement	5,910.00
1–Berkeley Scale by kind arrangement	732.00
1–Digital Computer Type PDP 8 by kind arrangement	16,570.00
1–Cable produced by kind arrangement (according to original agreement, to be returned to producer for further	

use, but due to breakage that is not possible)	312.70
1–Air-traffic-control Tape Recorder (officially confiscated)	— — — —
1–IBM Computer 707 by kind arrangement (paid for by bricks originally intended for the construction of a new laboratory)	— — — —
Manufacture of 1 (one) harness, by kind arrangement	3,012.12
Materials for resiliency meters, installations for measuring gravity, etc.	3,314.00
1–Loin-cloth	16.20
Total	Kčs 51,117.02

Honoraria:

Asst. Prof. Kastor Placenta (fee for supplying an Expert Opinion and the conducting of experiments, plus 10% surcharge for unusual difficulties)	Kčs 385.00
Professor Emerich Durych (fee for a scientific Dissenting Opinion)	3,000.00
Jakub Kubala, technician (remuneration for the construction of all remaining apparatuses outside regular working hours, see breakdown)	19,989.90
Dr. Šašinka (remuneration for programming the portable computer PDP 8)	50.00
Total	Kčs 23,424.90
Grand total	Kčs 74,541.92

[Note: The same files contain a notation of June 5, same year, by the accounting department of the Ministry of Justice in which a higher office is alerted that "in the case of Assistant

Professor Placenta the claimed surcharge for unusual difficulties is in no way justified, since the work was carried out
exclusively in dry and comfortable surroundings, providing
unobjectionable protection against weather and all other in-
clemencies. The sum of Kčs 35.00 is therefore regarded as
having been fraudulently obtained and legal proceedings are
being initiated for the recovery of same."]

PROPOSALS FOR INDICTMENT

submitted June 12, 19--, to the office of the Attorney General
by Edgar Blín, examiner.

Comrade Attorney General:
    In response to your inquiry regarding case No. 868–
12/19--, I should like to inform you that I have taken over the
case from Examiners Dr. Arnošt Salabák and Vilém Beran
on May 30 (that is, a day after my qualifying examination),
and, as it happened, at the point at which two mutually
contradictory Expert Opinions had been submitted but no
single indication of the shape the indictment is to take.
    In fulfilling my assignment I have taken energetic steps to
provide an immediate and effective remedy.
    Upon preliminary examination of both Opinions I found
that that by Assistant Professor Placenta was not only under-
pinned by extensive documentation but also coincided with
the results of my own inspection. For these reasons I have
excluded Professor Durych's Opinion from further consideration. While its loyalty is beyond question, it is utterly stupid.
    I have reached the decision to begin with the fact that
Accused XY does in fact overcome gravity and that he is able

to demonstrate that ability at any time in court, which could drive an indictment denying this fact into a corner.

In my view then the indictment must dispense with what was originally proposed by Dr. Arnošt Salabák, namely, Pars. 175 (false testimony), 199 (dissemination of false rumors), and 250 (fraud), and, on the contrary, base itself on the Accused being in fact able to exercise his talent. The fear that this may soften the indictment attests to the small degree of confidence placed in our Criminal Code, while a case like this, *precisely* a case like this, opens up a whole line of brilliant possibilities.

Section 1, Par. 1 of the Czechoslovak Criminal Law offers the opportunity of prosecuting under Par. 100 (sedition), according to which sedition consists in any act by which the perpetrator attempts to "call forth hostile feelings against protected objects," among which we certainly must count the law of gravity of Comrade Newton. In our case the condition of being a seditionist is also fulfilled "by inciting at least two individuals who are either simultaneously or sequentially present, namely individuals who are able to recognize sedition and understand it." An interesting, bold, and certainly unexpected solution would be the application of Par. 111, under the provisions of which fall violations of rules related to Law No. 147/1947 (agreement on international civil air traffic), the incursion of military aircraft and *other objects* into our air space, to which the quoted agreement does not refer. Worth noting is that the rule of Par. 111 is subsidiary to Par. 105 (espionage activities).

Examiners Dr. Salabák and Comrade Beran have also underestimated Section II (punishable acts of an economic nature) although we are plainly offered there Par. 116 (deprivation of goods serving the economy), which guarantees that "objects of value which derive from an *earlier* period and from the acts of former exploiters and the petit-bourgeoisie, and objectively represent *the fruits* of social labor in the past (to which undoubtedly belongs gravity), may be utilized in fulfilling the plans of the people's economy" in order for them not to be misused in speculative ventures (Par. 117).

An entire palette of magnificent charges is available in Section III (punishable acts against public order). In first place is Par. 164 (incitement) under which is subsumed every expression "designed to shake citizens' opinion concerning the reprehensibleness of certain acts and to awake and solidify a favorable attitude towards the commission of such acts." Pars. 169 and 170, on the other hand, pursue the "impairment and imperilment of the activities of public bodies and the bodies of social organization" (could also include the impairment of the syllabus in physics!) and Par. 171, "impairment of the execution of official decisions," which the Accused committed when he torpedoed the resolution of the special plenary session of the governing body of the town K. regarding the public retraction of his views by which he became accountable for the now well-known, but then unforeseeable, consequences. Last but not least there exists the possibility of applying Par. 177 (impairment of preparations for, and conduct of, elections), elections, which, as we know, did not in fact take place as a result of the mentioned developments.

In Section IV my predecessors overlooked Par. 181 (violation of duty during an acute emergency), the relevant point of which is that the culprit "impairs or renders more difficult the prevention or relief of an acute emergency by which at least a part of the population of a locality is affected." The lawmaker states specifically that this emergency "need not have been called into being by a general threat, nor need it be marked by general danger."

If the acute emergency is nevertheless marked by a general danger, which in our case is easily proved (e.g., the serious accident of my predecessor, Examiner Vilém Beran, who is at the moment hospitalized), "the herein described act will as a rule be punished more severely," that is, according to Par. 179 (public imperilment). I would not be afraid to apply

Pars. 189–192 (spreading of contagious diseases) even though —as shown in the tragedy of Comrade Beran—the consequences of AJ's doings would sooner fall under Section VII (aiding and abetting suicide).

Of course, enormous opportunities are opened by Section V (punishable acts which grossly violate public harmony), especially Par. 200, according to which the spreading of *all* rumors (even true ones) is punished by the Military Emergency Stand-by Corps (even in a State of Emergency!), in so far as rumors "bring about despondency in at least a part of the population of a locality," which again happens to fit our case. Moreover, I rather like Par. 209 in which the object of a punishable act are the *non-material* rights of individuals, that is, the right of a citizen to have the earth's gravity protected against centrifugal force caused by the rotation of the planets as well as by the condition of weightlessness and other conditions.

My predecessors also overlooked completely and unjustly Par. 217, Section VII (imperilment of the moral education of youth), an actual fact, which I would prove not only with the happenings in K., but also, if called upon, by testifying in my own case.

I am furthermore immensely attracted by Par. 249, Section IX (unauthorized use of others' effects) where according to sub-section (a) the culprit "appropriates something which was not in his possession before" or "uses it temporarily" by which is understood a use "that transgresses the limits of the culprit's authorization and impairs the actual purpose of its use," which in the overcoming of gravity is evidently the case.

Should the Attorney General's staff wish to make a public example to deter others by imposing the *severest* punishment possible, I propose, however, to invoke Section X (punishable acts against humanity), especially Par. 262 (use of prohibited weapons), also Section XI (punishable acts against defense forces), viz., Par. 266 (impairment of fitness for active duty), and finally Section XII (punishable acts of a military nature), Par. 284 (unauthorized separation) which speaks unambiguously of an "unauthorized absence without leave," which in an extended sense can easily be applied to the removal of the body of Accused from the earth's surface.

As for myself, Comrade Attorney General, I would personally, and in the first place, plead for invoking Par. 293 (insult to a truce negotiator). The security and honor of a negotiator and his escort are protected by this regulation. Negotiators are people whom the military leadership has commissioned to enter into negotiations in the theater of war with the military leadership of the enemy. A negotiator can be recognized by a white flag. As a rule, the flag is made of cloth. By cloth we mean any material that according to the preamble of the Fourth Hague Convention stands in opposition to customs prevailing between two civilized nations and to the laws of humanity and the requirements of public conscience (see Andrukhin, M.N., *Genocid: Tyagchaysheye Prestupleniye Protiv Chelovyechestva,* Gosyurisdat, Moskva, 1961). Public conscience is the basis of public care. The basic law is the attitude of mind. Ignorance of the law is no excuse. Ignorance today, crime tomorrow. Tomorrow dancing in the streets. Eastwest, home is best. Who laughs best, laughs last. Slast. Ast. Ssssst. St. T. A leeetle cAAAbin in the wooooods, leeetle marihuaaaaanaa by the window st-st-stooo-oood, ooood, oop, glug, yoohoooo, qry&789%***

[Note: the reason for the somewhat unusual recommendations of Examiner Edgar Blín, especially the astonishing conclusion, are contained in Reconstruction 10.]

RECONSTRUCTION 10

(According to contemporary records)

When at
midnight the gate of the detention jail of K. closed shut behind him, from which Comrade Nohýnek had already in the afternoon for safety's sake released all prisoners who unfortunately at once organized the demonstration consisting of *declassé* elements and others, which in turn necessitated the dispatch of police units and their renewed
arrest, they returned, pleasantly refreshed and without a single member missing, so that when he arrived at such a late hour, certain difficulties arose, he finally had to be offered a cell which was already occupied. It was No.
157, he laughed aloud when it occurred to him that coincidentally his hotel room had had the same number, the room in which he had
last slept, he exchanged a brief greeting with his cellmate and lay down immediately in order to gather strength for the coming battle, but there was a sudden desperate banging at the door, the other occupant pointed to the ceiling and crying begged the guard to transfer him to another cell because he was in custody as a petty
spy, at first they were going to remedy the situation by demanding that prisoner Juráček, in obedience to prison rules, lie on the bunk, but he turned himself over and went on sleeping with a cherubic smile as though he were on a soft pillow, they were afraid to wake him roughly because he might
fall. They put the spy in with the Siamese twins who had been accused of patricide, one twin accusing the other, and all night they kept watching the prisoner in cell No. 157, letting themselves in for a discussion in the course of which it almost came to
condoning the crime. He awoke in the morning fresh as

though new-born and fell in with prison life with such spirit that he might have been

born in the cell. Since that moment shortly before his arrest when he had decided to become an anti-Galileo and defend his truth, he knew that if he was going to defy power successfully he would first of all have to make his own a complete range of tricks and skills invented and perfected by entire generations of

underdogs, already at noon he gave away, though he himself still hadn't taken up smoking, aromatic cigarettes which were harmless and which he had rolled from toilet paper and filled with dried

white cabbage, a certain police lieutenant Mikeš escaped later to Holland, had it patented and busted with it the Westeuropean tobacco

cartel, at night they found him with a four-yard rope, woven from pieces of macaroni, true, he had been served rather tough macaroni that day, but no one ever imagined what stress it could bear when tested it broke only under the load of police sergeant Pelc who weighed 205

pounds, at night they were to discover that he was able to communicate by tapping on the wall as rapidly as they could by

telephone, they weren't even aware that he had developed an entirely new theory of communication according to which one single tap could mean a whole series of symbols, even words, he had started from the same principle as used by communication centers of news services in sending their messages by

coded impulses, unfortunately he was unable to complete his study for lack of an equally intelligent fellow

prisoner on the other side of the wall, and there was no time left to find one because a bare forty-eight hours in the district jail sufficed to convince the superior authorities that he was undermining the morale of the entire prison community, but most especially the guards who uninterruptedly assembled in front of his cell so that their inattention elsewhere allowed one of the Siamese twins to make his escape, some of them were even at work on a resolution to release him forthwith and appoint him advisor to the Minister of

Prisons, instead it was firmly concluded that the case demanded a higher court and the Municipal Criminal Court of

Prague was entrusted with it. The accused was transferred in the evening of March 23, to the new, until now unused, prison which had thoughtfully been erected at the confluence of the Vltava and Sázava, where in future Southtown was to rise, on the model of famed Spandau Prison he was going to be the sole prisoner for the time being, according to the experience of the detention jail in K. the guards were drawn from the bottom educational level, which caused a lot of

work, but there was no end to difficulties, the security officials entrusted with watching over the guards soon found out that some of the most reliable, pretending to their wives they had treated themselves to a mistress with whom they spent every free evening, had evidently under the influence of the prisoner started a correspondence course at the high

school, when a certain Pal'o Růžička, until recently impervious even to the ABC, was caught buying a slide rule, the whole squad was reassigned and in its place students were recruited for two months under a work agreement and for remuneration that took account of neither a tax on wages nor a tax on artistic endeavors, foreign

students, overwhelmingly from

Africa, chiefly such who had just arrived and therefore didn't know a word of

Czech, it was money wasted, but who would suspect that he was also a poly

glot, after learning the Pali-Maghadi dialect, Kurdish or Swahili gave him fewer difficulties than, for instance, Slovak with its soft

l, however, he was becoming more cautious, they had to

swear to him by all their gods, each student by each god, not to betray him, he was afraid he'd be assigned in their place —all good things come in three's—some deaf-and-

dumb guards, their fear of their gods' vengeance (all the gods at once) prevented betrayal, in fact, they kept their mouths shut, as it turned out, to their own advantage, when they later earned their doctorates or engineering degrees and returned to their own countries they all became

colonels and remembered tenderly their first teacher and first prisoner until their exe

cution which only the famous Nbongho-Nbongho escaped, the first Congolese astronaut, owing to the fact that he failed to return from outer space at the set time, whereupon they punished him by

firing him from a cannon. He taught them Czech so well that they were able to pass their knowledge in pristine quality on to their children, the famous globetrotter Gustav Havel nearly had a stroke twenty-five years later when after many hardships he discovered at the source of the Niger an unknown tribe of pygmies whose chieftain, squatting while engrossed in a certain cultist rite, exclaimed loudly:

"Kulevole, kulevole . . ."*

and immediately after rejoiced:

"Aznovakulevole, drž́tesipoklopcejedeteskopce. . . ."*

Of course they played "matrimony," a card game which Adam Juráček had picked up while still in detention in K., the grateful students repaid him by conveying surreptitious letters between him and his mother who lived with her brother František Hopner, she never actually saw the messengers, on the prisoner's instructions they left the messages on the doorstep which they approached almost naked in order to blend better into the

dark, they crept up so expertly that in January of the

*In both cases Czech exclamations which literally mean:
"Balls, you ox! Balls, you ox!"
"Ballsagainyouox, holdyourfliesitsdownhill!"

following year several women and girls of Xavírov were pleasantly surprised to be giving birth to healthy

black babies, the incensed husbands and lovers quite pointlessly set fire to a nearby warehouse where

bananas from Morocco were ripening. Talking to his guards, whether Czechs or foreigners, was far from being the main focus of his prison life. That of course was his examination but even it could not take the usual

form in view of the oddness of the case, above all because from the very beginning that one item was lacking without which one cannot very well proceed, namely, a regular, or if not regular, at least some kind of a

charge. As soon as Examiner Dr. Arnošt Salabák had studied the file, he applied for immediate

retirement, and the case was assigned to Vilém Beran, an old, hard-boiled realist who knew his way around and who had won fame by extracting a confession from a widely hunted mass murderer of female post office employees, a man caught accidentally in an as yet uncommitted theft of a carrier

pigeon, he saw in this case another grand opportunity, he laid down the condition that he would at first run his investigation as an observer, while the actual work was left to the

expert, when that was finished he would put the indictment in order and launch his crisp

hearing, he managed things so that the tried team of Placenta-Durych got on the case, the two were tied by mutual respect and an almost tender friendship ever since Placenta successfully defended his Ph. D. dissertation before Durych, his first student in thir

teen years, Adam Juráček instantly agreed to playing the guinea pig, he cooperated gladly and intelligently, not only because that was the shortest route to freedom, but also because he was flattered, like any discoverer, that at last

specialists were investigating his life's work, he had no

inkling that with every step he took on the ceiling he drove them another step to

despair to which, surprisingly enough, the first victim to succumb was Vilém Beran, up to now so stolid. When Assistant Professor Placenta handed him a copy of his Expert Opinion, he read it through and disappeared, days later he was discovered on the floor of the Grand Hotel's ballroom in K. with fifty-seven

fractures, he let it be known that he had attempted a re-enactment at the scene of the feat, after his recovery he founded one of the numerous anti-Newtonian sects which were then in fashion, whereupon they

locked him up. His successor was Examiner Edgar Blín, who asked to be assigned to the case in order to win his spurs by it, he was young, talented, impassioned, and ambitious, and a man of outstanding moral and physical conditioning, unfortunately he turned in two weeks into a hopeless

drug addict. Then arose a

vacuum into which forthwith stepped District Attorney Bondy, appointed by the Attorney General himself, only a day before the trial, when at last a dignified

solution had been found and agreed upon, literally five

minutes before the stroke of twelve, when those staff members who were in the know and carried responsibility, staff members belonging to the Ministry of Justice, to the Municipal Government, and to the Attorney General's office, resembled mum

mies, the one who contributed most to that state of affairs was the accused, not only because he spent more time on the ceiling than on the ground, but also and more important because he began to insist, at alarming frequency but alas justly, on legal provisions which in his case they had

violated. It was incredible. They had taken severe precautions that no literature on the subject should fall into his hands. When the guards went on duty they had to remove all their clothes and then make their rounds girded in nothing but oral messages, who would have thought that each had been given the daily assignment to recite from memory one

paragraph of the laws, after their oral delivery he reconstructed and memorized in less than a month the entire Code of

Criminal Procedure and the Criminal Code so that to the boundless astonishment and dismay of the court officials he rejected a defense lawyer *ex officio* and announced he was looking forward to presenting his own

defense, which made them look posthaste for a way out, after being in touch with the very highest authorities they found one and put it into effect, the trial was scheduled for Monday, the 21st of

June, to which the accused commented ironically that apparently it was a matter of an original observance of the anniversary of the execution of the Bohemian barons and he was wondering whether they'd at least give him the specifics of the indictment before the

execution, he was in

first-rate shape, he knew every word of his opening address by heart, he planned to rip the District Attorney into

shreds at the very outset, merely itemizing all the serious violations and transgressions committed by the examiners should last eighty-

five minutes, he looked with

confidence forward to his trial, yes, one might say, with the same elation almost that twenty-seven years ago he bestowed on the little ticket-punch, the shoulder-bag, and the visored cap, he asked them to bring him from

K. his dark suit and the tie given him by Kateřina Horová, he was very much hoping to see her beside his mother and Uncle František Hopner in the first row, they did as he

asked, at the time they were systematically at work trying to uncover a weakness in him and conceal the thinness of the ice they were treading, they wanted him to

feel secure, at which they succeeded, he suspected

nothing. Touched by his imminent transfer on the morning of June 21, he said good-bye to his faithful Africans and made a date to meet them at "The Jug" at six in the evening after the

trial, not realizing (he never read novels) that the idea was not wholly original.* He slept soundly, ate his breakfast with excellent appetite, he felt rested, fresh, and full of

self-confidence, he was delighted to be told that he would be tried in the main courtroom of the law buildings in the presence of delegates from all districts of the Republic. They had been selected by direct and secret vote that took the place of the originally planned election for various

representative offices, except for district K., still in a State of Emergency, where a delegate was appointed, namely, and in view of his old friendship with the accused, Director

Voráček, the accused felt even more heartened by this, he had once before experienced the shock of confronting the overcrowded ballroom and pictured himself, not without certain gloating, how today's audience would react when he would take his walk

on the ceiling of the courtroom, and what would be said about him and especially about the plaintiff by the representatives of an impatient electorate, that is why he was a little

taken aback, when they opened the door for him to a room, though huge and high-ceilinged, yet placed within it a narrow and low box of shatterproof

glass, at best able to accommodate a hand

stand, they assured him it had been done in regard to his safety, he saw through their low maneuver, but he

took courage again, he still had his

voice, he was connected to the rest of the world by micro-

*Good Soldier Schweik casually arranged for a rendezvous with rifleman Vodička in the same café, and, as it happened, at six P.M. after the war.

phones and loudspeakers, he was convinced that he would enforce proof of his

truth, he calmed himself, winked happily at his mother who actually did sit with her brother František Hopner in the first row, he did not see Kateřina Horová next to them, but that did not

upset him particularly, after all she was not a member of his

family,

he believed she was somewhere in the

courtroom, or at worst in front of a

television screen, he discovered not far from him the signal lights of TV cameras and blinked self-consciously into the lenses as he had seen it done on televised contests in figure

skating, he saw behind the impersonal lenses millions of eager eyes, and not suspecting that for security reasons they were merely video

taping him which, in case everything went according to plan, would be

put on the air only with the evening news, he conveyed to them by glances and gestures: well, good friends, I'll put on for you some of my free

style action. A loud clatter brought him up short, a hundred seats had flipped up because the judges were entering, he was aware that the presiding judge was by decree of fate a man of

unshakable principles who once during the period of lawlessness had to sentence an officer of the border guard for treason because he had told a foreign tourist the quickest route to

Prague, shortly before the sentencing he disappeared, he lived like a modern-day Tarzan for more than ten years in a marshy wood, by himself, among

wild boars whose itching, hardened clumps of mud he scraped off for which they rewarded him with beechnuts, perhaps he would never have found out about the sweeping changes, which

altered society for the better, had he not accidentally been shot by a poacher, since then he enjoyed widespread affection, a further reason for the accused to be more than satisfied. He did not know, as the presiding judge did not know, that this too was part of the plaintiff's

strategy, with a calm

conscience he resumed his seat, the severe frown on the presiding judge's forehead hinted of how he was going to whip into the

District Attorney for having taken it upon himself to submit in lieu of an indictment such a preposterous

travesty Let it be said clear and plain that the presiding judge had meant to proceed along this line, after all he had not kept it secret from the District Attorney, he had informed him that although the government had the right to declare a deed a hundred times over a threat to society, nevertheless it had simultaneously the duty to

offer proof, and he had expressly drawn his attention to the fact that he was not going to put up with any

monkey-business but offer this young man every legal

opportunity by which he might

defend himself, which in the face of an

indictment at this

level presumably wasn't a

problem. When the District Attorney held his ground with his indictment, he had ominously shrugged his shoulders and left for the courtroom in order to carry out his duty, he threw the accused a searching glance and felt about the cramped aquarium as the

latter did, namely, that they would soon liberate him from it so he might show what he

could do, then he turned to the first page of the deplorable document, rounded his lips to utter the opening

words, from a
row of seats rose a
shout, he raised his eye
brows and discovered, like all the other eye
witnesses, not excluding the accused behind the glass, nor
excluding the camera eyes,
a corpulent, middle-aged man in the audience who was
jabbing at the bare ceiling and without letup was hysterically
screaming:
"There, there, he's walking again, walking again!"

COMMENTS

by the Chief Television News Commentator on the taped trial of the Accused AJ, broadcast on June 21, 19--, at 7:06 P. M.

(In color)

All of you good friends out there watching tonight!

The true-to-life scenes you have just witnessed on your screens have caught the last act but one of what I would call a human tragicomedy.

Although in essence we have not commented on the events that took place in March of this year in K., conforming to the sensible desire of most of you, dear and respected viewers, who did not want to be wrenched from your workaday lives by tawdry sensationalism—we nevertheless have no intention of denying that those events called forth unusual measures and thus a certain interest.

What has actually happened?

Today, as things have become all too clear, a brief

recapitulation cannot do harm to anyone in any way.

At the beginning of March this year, more precisely on Thursday the 4th of that month, AJ, a hitherto unknown Professor of Physical Education and Drawing at a school in K., set out to claim that he had learned how to overcome the force of earth's gravity, and at that—listen to this, will you —by will power.

Let's get this much straight:

A strong will belongs among those qualities which we obviously wish to infuse in our children for their family life, their school work, and their occupations. But we have never placed it in defiance of universally valid laws of nature. The days of idealistic oh-if-it-were-only-so philosophies are long past—and modern society is not prepared to tolerate the shenanigans of private witch-doctors who put forward the claim, for example, of being able to stop dead in its tracks a roaring locomotive by means of will power.

If they could, there wouldn't be dozens of individuals killed every year due to malfunctioning of railroad barriers.

What startles is that this ludicrous, albeit dangerous, claim was propagated by a professor and even by the officials of the town K. who threw the public into confusion with the further claim that they had witnessed with their own eyes the accused AJ's levitation.

A public meeting arranged for Sunday, March 21, at a certain hotel crowned the whole affair. That is when the mentioned performance was watched by allegedly more than a thousand townspeople. The disorders that were immediately created by *declassé* elements and others compelled the government to take the justified and readily understood step which every sensible citizen would warmly second, even though it brought along certain economic privations which every one of us felt in his pocketbook.

That explains the great suspense awaiting the public trial in which the elected representatives of all our country's districts participated. The citizens demanded rightfully that an end be put to rumors and that truth and justice should forge a tunnel into the open.

What happened in the very first minute of the trial dispelled all confusion, even if in a truly shocking manner.

A man rose from among the audience and began to scream that AJ was once again walking on the ceiling, whereas it was clear to everyone including you, dear and respected viewers, conclusively clear, that the accused was visibly sitting in his assigned place from which he could not physically remove himself because he was hermetically sealed in a box of shatterproof glass.

Then and there an attempt was made to identify the man who had caused the uproar. The attempt was made by the presiding judge, Dr. Vorel, generally acclaimed for his absolute fairmindedness which he had demonstrated during a certain painful period of certain temporary lawlessness, fortunately done away with once and for all by what came after. The astonishing result was this:

It was the Director of the Pedagogical Institute of K. and the old friend of the accused, Bohuslav Voráček, that is, the same Voráček who was the most vociferous witness in behalf of AJ's alleged upward floating, that is—will wonders never cease?—a three-time witness.

The trial was called off at once, and the judges withdrew to deliberate. In the course of the day a series of leading experts were consulted in turn, but this time there were no physicists among them, only psychologists and psychiatrists.

What was it all about?

Dear and respected viewers, without wishing to prejudge the case in the least, let alone interfere in the still unresolved court proceedings which may last until the small hours of the night, if not longer—

one thing seems to be certain:

This morning's events bear witness to the fact that Director Voráček, and with him professors, officials, inhabitants, and the young people of the town and district of K., have fallen prey to one of the most bizarre cases of mass hypnosis in the recorded annals of mankind.

Yes, respected viewers and dear friends, as you yourselves saw a minute ago on your screens, the celebrated conqueror of gravity AJ did not leave the solid ground for even a fraction of a second to perform his breakneck circus stunt!

What needs to be added?

Perhaps this, that it is now the task of experts and judges to decide whether he consciously perpetrated his hocus-pocus to make money and to shake the confidence of our people in a materialistic world view, or—and this cannot yet be excluded if we do not want to be cast back into ages of despotism—whether he has the unconscious power of hyp-notism. However, this would in no way amount to a super-natural manifestation but, on the contrary, be explainable, as it has been explained by a whole series of well-known world travellers and doctors, for instance, among Indian fakirs.

Anyway, respected friends and dear viewers, we won't have to wait long for the result, and in either case we can rest assured that as of today we are poorer by one mirage.

Our good luck!

The inhabitants of the town and district of K. will breathe easier because this afternoon the unpleasant State of Emer-gency has been lifted. The careworn physics instructors will breathe easier, and so will we parents breathe easier because our misled children will surely once again trust us when we say that the life we live is not one of walking about on the ceiling but diligent study and doing honest work.

And should anyone among us regret that he failed to be a contemporary of an epoch-making event, then let him remind himself that it was our lot to suffer through two wars and that it was in our own lifetime that men took their first steps on the moon. That it will never be by suggestion and hypnosis but simply and solely by the concrete efforts of progressive politicians, scientists, technicians, and workers that will, without the little Czech gym and drawing teacher, make the vision of the poet come true who says:

> We strike at the bars, we lionhearted,
> And shall smash them!

LAST WILL AND TESTAMENT

of Bohuslav Voráček, Director of the Pedagogical Institute in K., June 23, 19--.

My beloved children,

You are still too young to understand your unhappy father, and yet old enough to judge him. I do not blame you, I merely remind you that it is your hard words that drive me into the arms of nothingness. I have decided to leave you my last letter so that when you are grown you will realize how cruelly you have done me an injustice.

As you do today, so I too, beloved children, once had dreams and ideals. A few recent literary attempts which I put on paper at the end of last winter, though under another name, will confirm to you that I possess an undeniable talent for fiction. I do not exaggerate when I say that it could have helped me to highest distinction.

This talent I sacrificed for you, my beloved children, when I placed above my personal ambitions a difficult duty when only a senior in high school and as a young man on the threshold of life: I married your mother whom I hated even when she was still my teacher. Nonetheless I married her for love, for love, that is, for what was going to be born, and that was you. Thanks to the sad fact that I behaved like a decent person and did not urge your mother to an abortion, I have prevented multiple murder.

And so I sacrificed to the four of you not only my youthful ideals but also my years of ripeness, my beloved children. Instead of teaching my favorite subjects of Czech and Geography, I voluntarily took on the yoke of Director of the Institute, of which I will presently have more to say.

Today you threw the name of Jan Hus in my face and accused me of betraying truth, friends, family, hometown, fatherland, and the progress of all mankind. You declared, my beloved children, that your father is literally a coward and a liar.

Though I have decided to draw from that the only possible consequence, tragic for me as well as for you, my dear children, I hope I still have enough moral credit left, after your tears have replaced your anger, that you will listen to my reasons.

I deny at the outset that they were utilitarian and purely self-serving. I have already shown you that your very existence, beloved children, speaks for my character. However paradoxical it may sound, I did it exclusively for your sake, for the sake of my school, our town and all of society.

You maintain that Adam Juráček spoke the truth and proved it. That you not only watched it with your own eyes, but that marks of his shoes remain on several ceilings, thus contradicting the official version. Perhaps you do speak the truth. Yes, let us assume he did actually speak the truth. But then he spoke it prematurely, my beloved children. Truth must wait for the right moment. And a premature truth is under certain circumstances worse than a lie.

Truth as such, truth in itself, as they put it so well, pure truth, does not in truth exist, since it is exclusively the product of idealistic thinking. Truth is manifold and often self-contradictory. Each person has his own truth, says the famous dramatist. Even the bourgeois has one, my dear children. For all that, we were always concerned with—

myself and, I believe, you too—with truthful truth.

What kind of truth is that, I ask you. Despite youthful intolerance, you must admit that there is still one thing I master better than you, namely Czech and Geography. The true truth was, is, and will be only that which serves Czech Geography, whereas the untrue truth harmed it and harms it, my beloved children.

Just take a look at the map of the Bohemian states through their history, my dear children. Jan Hus, whom you led into battle against me, became a popular folk martyr only because by his truth the borders of our country were pushed deep into Germany, Hungary and the Baltic territories. In contrast, the Bohemian classes who in 1618 defenestrated imperial officials could not have been in possession of truth since the Kingdom of Bohemia slipped for three hundred years on to the map of Austro-Hungary.

What kind of a truth, I now ask you, has Adam Juráček expressed with his doings? Mine? Yours? That of our people, my beloved children? Could these hard-pressed people of ours run the risk of losing their borders altogether? Did they not run the danger that the territory they thus disdained would be occupied by superpowers who would leave them only the ceilings to live with? Can you perhaps picture what a future atlas and globe would have looked like?

Not I, my beloved children. Should I have had my hand in that disaster merely because I happened by pure chance to be Juráček's friend and happened to witness his crazy doings?

Just the opposite. It was thus, dear children, thus and not otherwise that I was fated to give false testimony, especially as I was also told I could else not keep my post as Director of my beloved school, my beloved children.

I could not run the risk, my beloved children, that my place should be taken by an oppressor of the true truth. And I could not run the risk of depriving you, my beloved children, of the living standard you deserve and of that spring-board into life and society.

However preposterous it may seem to you today, my dear children, the fact remains that the stormy years of youth fade away and the young revolutionaries are warmly grateful to their fathers that they have helped them to a secure post with their savings, their connections, their solicitude, my beloved children, their name and their sacrifices.

Then perhaps you too, my beloved children, will grasp that my sacrifice was one of the most difficult.

My beloved children!

If you assert that Jan Hus and Adam Juráček were heroes in contrast to your beloved father, because they defended the *known* truth, then it shall serve me as an additional ex-cuse that not since I can remember have I personally come across truth; the one time I did see it, I saw right through it.

All the more does your unjust verdict, my beloved chil-dren, pain me. My life means nothing to anyone any longer, and that is why I leave it. I say good-bye to you in the hope that this gesture, this irreversible gesture, will convince you of your wretched father's honesty, my dear, beloved chil-dren.

Good-bye.

[Note: This Last Will and Testament was handed to the press by Voráček's widow the day after the funeral, as she expressly notes in her own Last Will. It is all the more peculiar that both were only recently discovered in the ar-chives of the Ministry of the Interior. The subsequent fate of Bohuslav Voráček is uncommonly interesting. Although the day following AJ's trial the Ministry of Education decreed that all individuals prone to hypnosis or suggestion were relieved of their professional duties respecting the education of young people studying or working—affected were Professors Vilibald Bláha, Sováková, Krbálek, and twelve other members of the faculty of the Pedagogical Institute in K., in addition, some hundred teachers and intellectuals from all parts of the country—Voráček was immediately appointed District Inspector of Schools in P. and a year later even deputy to Madame Minister of Education. This was after he had married her mother, a move made possible for him by the tragic decease of his first wife who had inexplicably locked herself in the refrigerator with the door facing the wall. He himself died only five years later due to cirrhosis of the liver. He did not go through with the suicide announced in his Last Will because, acting on erroneous information, he had placed himself on a disused siding and was rescued two days later. The funeral mentioned at the beginning of this note referred to his children—quadruplets who wilfully pulled the brand-new monument to the great Newton down on themselves. The monument was put up again and for safety's sake surrounded with a terrarium full of reptiles in order to forestall a repetition of like incidents. Inexpert care, however, led to the reptiles' chronic undernourishment: so they helped themselves. After the wife of a diplomat of a friendly nation, walking in the arcade, and being small and round and unfortunately dressed in a coat of rabbit fur— after she was swallowed by a giant python, it was decided to do away with the terrarium and replace it with an impenetrable thicket. It would be apropos to think about fixing up a place that reverentially recalls the life drama of AJ.]

VERDICT

in the Name of the Republic

After the trial held on June 23, 19--, the Criminal Court of Prague arrived at the following

Verdict.

Accused Adam Juráček, born on December 24, 19--, in K., last resident in K., 1 Park Street, lately Professor of Physical Education and Drawing at the Pedagogical Institute in K.,

is acquitted

of the charge of committing punishable acts according to Par. 118 (unauthorized exercise of a professional activity), Par. 123 (unauthorized disposition of an invention), Pars. 136 and 137 (damage to socialist property), Par. 149 (unfair competition), Par. 205 (corruption of morals), Par. 209 (impairment of foreign rights), Par. 236 (interference with freedom of religion), Par. 238 (breach of domestic peace), Par. 257 (damage to foreign property), Par. 258 (misuse of property), Pars. 273 and 274 (refusal to obey commands) of the Criminal Code, because he deviated from the law of gravity without being entitled or empowered to do so and thereby *de facto* broke it.

Substantiation:

By hearing witnesses and consulting with numerous experts it was clearly demonstrated that Accused committed no punishable acts according to Pars. 118, 123, 136 and 137, 149, 205, 209, 236, 238, 257, 258, as well as Pars. 273 and 274 of the Criminal Code, because all his supposed feats and the punishable acts related thereto did not take place in actuality but exclusively in the imagination of the world around him as a result of a so-called mass-hypnosis called forth by the suggestive powers of the Accused. Since it could not be proved that Accused consciously worked hypnosis, but since it is rather a psychic characteristic owing its existence to the physical make-up of Accused, it can be taken as proved that Accused could not on account of his psychic disturbance recognize how his deed threatened society, nor could he control the above-mentioned capacity. He is therefore in the meaning of the law, Par. 13, sub-section 1, Criminal Code, on the basis of mental derangement, legally not responsible. But since Accused despite honest attempts continued to exert hypnotic effects on experts and judges during the examination and trial, and successfully so, and since it must therefore be assumed that his remaining at liberty will not be without danger and may lead to unforeseeable consequences, the court decided that Accused Adam Juráček, according to Par. 72, subsection 1, Criminal Code (see No. 31/34 Compendium of Decisions in Criminal Law) is to undergo

preventive medical treatment.

SANATORIUM ASSIGNMENT

by the Court Medical Examiner, June 23, 19--.

To the Psychiatric Sanatorium Na Brodě in Southern Bohemia:

According to today's decision by the Court, citizen Juráček Adam, born December 24, 19--, in K., was declared unfit. Your sanatorium is entrusted with his preventive medical treatment.

According to findings, citizen J. Adam has evinced since childhood psychic instability which degenerated into extreme depression and extreme euphoria. By simulating a work accident the father of J. Adam committed an adroit suicide in order to fraudulently extract from his employer financial support for his family. Moreover, it was ascertained that, feigning for decades the role of a decent working widow, the mother of J. Adam demolished last night, manifestly under the influence of alcohol, the clock in the Old City town hall, claiming it was a cuckoo-clock stolen from her.

Beginning March 4, of this year, J. Adam compelled the world around him to believe that he was able to overcome gravity. This eventuated in a series of private and social upheavals.

In the course of his examination, J. Adam is anywhere from defiant to arrogant, he stares fixedly at doctor and staff and influences them by hypnosis to favor his claims. Aware of place, time, and persons, he raises objections against having been illegally deprived of his freedom and demands that the officials of the Public Health Ministry, of the Court, and of the Government should undergo psychiatric treatment in his place.

As to his physical state, there are no pathological changes, the tongue has no coating, EKG and X-ray are normal, temperature is 98.6, pulse 80 p/min., blood pressure 120/85 mm Hg.

J. Adam resisted transfer, for which reason he was given pentathol 0.22 intravenously. I recommend admission to the restricted section of your sanatorium to implement the treatment ordered by the Court.

Dr. [*signature illegible*]

RECONSTRUCTION 11

(According to contemporary records)

When the first tw
elve months had elapsed since the gate of the cloister Na
Brodě had fallen shut behind him, which he had not entered
on his own free will but by delivery on government orders,
for the dour complex in an entrancing landscape had long
fulfilled the function of a psychiatric institution, delivered, in
fact, in a straitjacket which in his pentathol daze he had
taken for the embrace of Kat
eřina Horová, the Medical Direct
or Polonyi was notified that a commission from Prague
was enroute to settle the ensuing fate of this luckless man
because of a medical report. Polonyi was his con
temporary but he resembled somehow the hotheaded examiner Edgar Blín before he turned into a notorious drug
addict, chiefly owing to his spi
rit and straightforward thinking, Polonyi often and
proudly asserted that, though a doctor, he was first and
foremost a doctor of the human soul, still no in
tellectual, in his interminable conversations with this patient whom he grew so fond of that the latter nearly replaced
his beautiful and passionate wife who had refused to share
his bed in a former cloister cell far removed from the capital,
more
over, share it with madmen among whom she also counted
her hus
band, by which she painfully reminded her husband of an
anonymous girl whose composite portrait emerged from the
cries of the patients, that too brought him closer to this
patient. Treating Juráček, he ac
tually treated himself, it helped him to determine on the
spot the cause of the disease and to fill in the blank on the
Medical Court Examiner's admittance form, he looked upon

that form as the work of an irresponsible dilettante, sim

ply of an intellectual who was incapable of thinking logically and therefore unable to arrive at a diagnosis even though it prac

tically stared him in the face, and the face was the ceiling. If instead of the newfangled rubbish, the Medical Court Examiner had from time to time glanced at the old textbooks, then he would, like Medical Director Polonyi, have known that the desire to walk on the ceiling is a classical symptom of para

noia, Juráček displayed in an uncommon but demonstrable fashion all three of its major configurations, *paranoia inventoria,* inventor mania, *paranoia reformatoria,* mania to enlighten others, and *purunola querulatoria,* the delusion of suffering

injustice, it had not dawned on the medical court virtuoso that the *idée fixe,* namely, to overcome gravity by means of will power, was nothing but the quite well-known attempt to discover the *per*

petuum mobile, Juráček's idea was even more absurd, which indicated the presence of para

phrenia, in which, as every textbook points out, the delusions of realistic possibilities are noticeably far apart and the patient furthermore has the tendency to dissimulate, so that the doctor has no other choice than to ferret out his delusions and hallucinations, indeed to pro

voke them so that he should have something to

treat, this is also what he had to do in the case of Juráček who recuperated in an admirably short time from the shock occasioned by his friend Voráček's outcry, by the unexpected verdict, and by the straitjacket, he carried himself in the sanatorium in a way that made the first impression of a perfectly nor

mal person, certainly more normal than, for instance, the male head nurse Celestýn, who had been arrested several times in attempts at illegal crossing of national borders, although he had a valid passport, inci

dentally, he crossed the border in the direction of his home

land, or Dr. Mudr's assistant, who gave his nights to constructing a complex and expensive apparatus to produce fresh plums from Jelinek's sliv

ovitz, it was otherwise with Adam Juráček, the unexpected encircling move of his opponent confused him, who knew neither falseness nor pretense, confused him to such a degree that after the briefest resistance he essentially believed him, he felt remorse and shame and was ready to do everything on his part to be rid of the painful suffering, right from the first conversation with the Medical Director he himself admitted that to deny gravity only an i

diot would do, which he had almost become but did not intend to remain, at the very thought of his bewildered students he renewed his oath to the great Newton in such a touching and credible fashion that nothing remained for Polonyi to do but to have re

course to a stratagem, in the course of several weeks he gained his confidence, learned from him the basics of drawing and later even how to do the high jump, but at the moment at which he finally failed to clear 212 centimeters in the cloister's hothouse, he confidentially divulged to the patient that he too thought of gravity as the scourge of mankind, the stratagem suc

ceeded, Juráček opened up and took all night to describe to him, oath or no oath, his technique, at last Polonyi had him whe

re he wanted him, he could explain to him that his idea was nothing but the fruit of a distorted, false, inverted relationship to reality based on an ultraparadoxical phase and a pathological flaccidity which makes its appearance especially in the secondary level of con

sciousness, when he went

on to expound the fundamentals of biological therapy

which would be his quickest help, his despairing, annihilated charge gave his con

sent, and thus Polonyi could at last start on his actual treatment, by a con

catenation of circumstances exactly on the 4th of

September in the morning, half a year and half an hour after the time when in the resort section of K., in 1 Park Street, Mrs. Josefa Juráčková, born Hopnerová, widow of the train conductor, had opened the door to her son's room and had dropped her

tray. In view of the oddness and degree of the disease the doctor could hardly assume that a single treatment would do the job, so he decided on a whole panorama of treatments, and as a matter of fact in the chronological order in which medical science had brought them to light, he approached his task with possibly greater excitement than the pa

tient, the treatment he concocted resembled a ritual, it was to be something like a psy

chiatric celebration of the mass, in order to exalt the truly classical techniques he began, if only for the sake of experiment, with the method of the shepherd Melampus who approximately three hundred years before Homer was supposed to have freed the daughters of King Proitos from their delusion they were

cows, he made Juráček drink a decoction of hellebore and chased him across the meadows surrounding the cloister until he reached a point of exhaustion from which he barely recovered, but diarrhea, vomiting, pallor, dizziness, chills, and an epileptic attack with cramps, in short, everything designed to remove a psychic disturbance, though effectively called forth, struck, God knows why, not the patient but Polonyi him

self, that is why, when convalescence was over, he chose a less drastic but not less legendary procedure, constructed on the example of the biblical David's harp-playing before the melancholy Saul, but this musical therapy had to be cut short after numerous inmates, until then entirely harmless, crashed through the wall of the cloister and fled to the po

lice station where they demanded protection and claimed the Medical Director wanted to drive them

mad, the unwelcome attention of the police was the reason that he had to dispense with the excellent techniques of the Brahmins who released poisonous but toothless snakes to the insane on the assumption that their terror of being bitten would jar their psychic condition, and he had to dispense with

the sham executions effected by cutting the heart from the living body, according to the repertoire of the ancient Aztecs, so with

flogging, referred to by Esquirol in the famous work *Des Maladies Mentales,* further

more, the warmly recommended firing of a can

non in a patient's immediate vicinity, detailed in Johann Christian Reil (1759–1813),

Rhapsodies on the Application of Psychic Treatments for the Insane (1803), so in a trice he had to take recourse to more recent methods against which the police could raise no objections. In order to o

pen for Juráček the door to the inner shrine of modern shock therapy, he began, naturally, with cardiazol, which takes its name from pentamethylentetrazol, and which in 1930 the renowned von Meduna began to inject in his patients, based on the view current then but today entirely repudiated, about the incompatability of schizophrenic attacks and epi

lepsy, he tried out azoman shock (after von Braunmüller), shock caused by doses of ammonium chlorate (Bertolani's method), the acetylcholine shock (after Fiamberti), and the pyramidon shock (after C. Riebeling), popular in Germany in 1944 as there was a relatively small amount of in

sulin available for a relatively large number of insane, he continued with pneumo shock (after J. Delay), rather drastic for the patients, but of uncommon interest to the doctor as far as research is concerned, especially for throwing more light upon a given feeling or the effectiveness of shock therapy upon the diencephalic region, until at last he reached insu

lin shock (the introduction of which by the Viennese school of Manfred Sakel is most frequently contested), in general the most successful, but of no profit to Juráček, still Polo

nyi became witness to the only extant case of insulin resistance, since he succeeded only with a super dose of 12,500 units i.v. to induce in Juráček signs of at least a mild hypoglyccmia, which exceeded by five times the world famous experience of Rivers and Eliot, described in Bel

lack's *Dementia Praecox,* it was to be Polonyi's bad luck to come to grief before he found the time to discover his own Bellack, so that this record was never confirmed by anyone, never officially listed in ta

bles, and therefore all the less re

cognized The first successful results were produced by electric shocks after U. Cerletti (Cerletti & Bini) who on a casual walk through the Roman slaughterhouse in 1938 convinced himself that an animal felled by electric shock was not dead but had been struck by e

lectric e

pilepsy and therefore used electric shock in April of the same year in therapy, of course in much smaller dosages than for cattle, of psy

chopaths, so the first successful results showed up already after a few hundred impulses which Dr. Polonyi thrust into his patient's skull as long as the power supply of the district permitted it, being at winter's end rather

low, Adam Juráček began to show a truly exemp

lary apathy, became passively tractable, and his ever-increasing mental disturbances began to appear, especially as far as recent memories were concerned, in reply to control questions he stated that his name was

"Ráček or something like that . . ."

and he said about his feat that he had "tried to overcome something, maybe some kind of a record," in order to prevent a relapse and to speed up the effects of his treatment, the Medical Director combined electric shocks with pyre

totherapy, he inoculated the patient with malaria (after Dr. Rosenblum's Odessa experiments of 1860–1870) and drove the fever attacks—granted, with some risk—to 42° Centigrade, when he slowed them down with quinine, after the fading of the forty-ninth attack, the patient imagined he was called only

"Ček . . ."

and knew of his achievement merely that he "had tried something," Polonyi turned quickly to pharmaceutical

therapy, he began with the inhalation of carbon dioxide (also after von Meduna) and came to the therapeutic experiments of Wagner-Smitt of 1950 in which, by inhaling nitrogen, anoxia with loss of consciousness is caused, this technique was favorably put forward in the medieval treatment of the insane whereby the head was forcibly immersed in water for the length of time it took to say a Mi

serere, so that at last he could triumphantly proclaim that his charge, though unfortunately suffering from a few side effects caused by the treatment, among o

thers from advanced hypoglycemia, obstructions in the corneal and pupillary reflexes, disturbances in the vestibulary (and therefore also in its passage), of anemia, pneumonia, and lung gangrene (a pretty common consequence of electric shocks), of fracture of vertebrae Nos. 3 through 7 as well as of the left shoulder blade and thighbone, of dislocation of the upper arm and lower jawbone, and of biting through his

tongue, in addition to a certain reduction in weight from an original 154 pounds to 108 pounds, where

as of his name and his achievement he remembered zero point

zero, it was just then that the arrival of the commission was announced that was to come to a fresh decision in regard to Juráček's future. Whether it was to com

plicate his successful treatment for the sake of the commission, the Medical Director safeguarded his work by concluding with a drug therapy, he put his patient to sleep with a strong combination of chlorpromazine, methazine, and hibernon and kept him in an uninterrupted deep sleep for the remaining eleven

weeks, the period by which the arrival of the commission was unexpectedly delayed. When Polonyi's bell rang, served by a psychopath who lived in the delusion that the cloister was about to be attacked by Hus

site troops, he walked towards them through that part of the cloister where the mild cases were quartered, and it occurred to him that he had neglected them for almost a year because of Juráček, but immediately following, elation overcame him, the feeling of a champion of science who had single

handedly fought a victorious battle, the feeling did not leave him for a moment as he conducted the small troop of strutting intellectuals into his treatment room where the invalid, just awakened, was receiving light nourishment in small doses in order to prevent an overload of his gastrointestinal system after having "coast

ed" such a long time. Then after he reported that his experiment had been one hundred percent successful and proposed Juráček's release for home treatment, and after they still weren't enthused, in fact, everything but, he credited their reaction to the normal en

vy of such characters.

"Well, dear Colleague," said the chairman of the inspection commission, the Deputy Minister for Public Health,

Assistant Professor Kapr, "well, that was a respectable piece of work, but why—ahem!—is the patient in such a state . . . ?"

"Comrade Deputy Minister," said Dr. Polonyi pained, "excuse me but if a patient cooperates as willingly as this one has done and with such striking success, I don't see why he shouldn't be rewarded by stretching himself quietly
on the ceiling."

PERSONAL LETTER

from the Deputy Minister of Public Health, Assistant Professor Stanislav Kapr, to Assistant Professor Miloš Makovec-Smith&Wesson, July 20, 19--.

Asst. Prof. Miloš Makovec-Smith&Wesson,
Chief of the Psychiatric Clinic of the Medical Faculty,
Charles University, Prague,
Professor at the Smith & Wesson Psycho-Cybernetic Private Clinic
of Oklahoma City, Oklahoma.

Dear Colleague and Friend,

Since I discovered that you have returned to your country planning to train our future army of psychiatrists and at the same time complete your Ph.D. dissertation (which, I don't have the least doubt, will ensure you membership in the Academy), I turn to you with an urgent plea for help.

In our secluded sanatorium Na Brodě a patient has for many months been unsuccessfully treated, a patient whose name would mean nothing to you. Nevertheless it is the man who a year ago created the turmoil in K., of which you will undoubtedly have heard on the other side of the ocean, since it made a very unfavorable impression on world opinion. And at that, only the political aspects were played up since we fortunately succeeded in keeping the truth secret.

I may—no: I must—tell you in confidence: the truth consisted in this, that our man translated into actual practice the early literary invention in H. G. Wells' story "The Truth About Pyecraft" so much admired by us. I don't have to tell you more!

While the court reached the conclusion that our man hypnotized his audiences and witnesses, those experts, on the other hand, who keep an eye on the case—myself not excluded—are agreed that he actually does overcome gravity (and at that, more and more frequently), so that at most he hypnotizes himself.

I surely do not have to tell you what the consequences would be of reopening the case and the eventual confirmation of the facts, which were only so recently disproved by scientific, propagandistic, judicial, and political means and which required a whole series of measures by administrative and other cadres. The interests of society—and not only ours: I am convinced it is society in the largest sense of the word—demand that the trouble be explained and, more crucial, be eliminated.

As I have been an enthusiastic follower of your work, I am aware that you have dealt at depth with the dehypnotizing of the human personality. I believe that your Institute, and more particularly your personal care, will not only help this unfortunate individual, who is threatened by lifelong isolation, but also solve for you a problem of immense moral interest.

I am empowered to inform you that the highest authorities will not skimp on such means as promise to transform the Psychiatric Clinic into the most up-to-date establishment of the University. I tell you privately that the resolution of this task would be an achievement already now assuredly worth the national award in medicine; it will of course be necessary to devise a rationale which will not excite any undue domestic or world-wide attention.

I send you my warmest greetings, and think often and tenderly of our childhood games, and in conclusion beg you urgently to destroy this letter carefully after you've read it.

Your old fellow student and friend,
Standa Kapr

[Note: Assistant Professor Miloš Makovec acquired his unusual name by a shotgun marriage to the daughter of the famous arms manufacturer Smith & Wesson, a girl he seduced while she did her military service as interpreter at the First Film Festival in Karlsbad after the war. As a payoff both fathers-in-law established for him in Oklahoma a flourishing private clinic, which, however, he decided to leave as soon as he discovered that he was falling professionally behind his colleagues at home, who had the opportunity to examine more, and much more interesting, psychopaths than the relatively de-neuroticized Wild West was producing. His fathers-in-law released him from his contract on the condition that he would continue to use his new name for advertising purposes in his own country, a name he had acquired by marriage. At the same time, he stipulated divorce as a quid pro quo. After reading the above letter he destroyed a love note while he sent the Deputy Minister's letter to his student Uta Nováková. That is why she did not appear at the sex-garden-party for unattached doctors, but instead was years later able to produce this exceptionally valuable piece of evidence.]

MEMORANDUM

by Assistant Professor Miloš Makovec-Smith&Wesson, January 15, 19--.

Dear Standa,

I want to thank you for the greatest exhilaration that it has been my pleasure to experience in my scientific (and sexual!) career. Also I ask you to forgive me that the job took longer than we both thought and swallowed up more money than your bosses envisaged. But the result is worth it. I do not hesitate to call it prodigious!

It took me almost a year until I could get our man into a state reasonably close physically and psychologically to that in which he was before the psychiatric orgies hatched by my predecessor took place. I hope sincerely that meanwhile you have thrown this Polonyi to the wolves so that he's felt on his own body at least one of his favorite shocks.

It took another year before our man and I were able to communicate on the same wavelength, a precondition re garded as absolutely fundamental in modern American psychiatric practice. Only then could I approach my actual task.

I proceeded from the highly interesting study of my American colleague and friend, Maxwell Maltz, M.D., F.I.C.S., who in his *Psycho-Cybernetics* (Wilshire Book Company, 12015 Sherman Road, No. Hollywood, California 91605) literally states: "It is no exaggeration to say that every human being is hypnotized to some extent, either by ideas he has uncritically accepted from others, or ideas he has repeated to himself or convinced himself are true. These negative ideas have exactly the same effect upon our behavior as the negative ideas implanted into the mind of a hypnotized subject by a professional hypnotist" (Chapter entitled "Dehypnotize Yourself," p. 49).

Maxwell Maltz reaches the conclusion that the most

harmful self-hypnosis driving people into depressions and forthwith into hysterical behavior consists in their uncritical efforts to transform themselves into certain individuals who amount to something and, respectively, to become more famous than they. The tragedy of our man consists in that none other has "hypnotized" him than the great Newton.

Maxwell Maltz sees a solution in a kind of "anti-hypnosis." The doctor is to get the patient not to torture himself any longer by that in which he cannot equal the other, but he should, on the contrary, develop that in which he does equal him. In the case of our man, Maltz's method proved, however, a total failure. Had I followed it I would have got him to develop a capacity which it was my task to eradicate. In all modesty I hit upon something marvellous:

Our man was hypnotized by the desire to be the first man to overcome earth's gravity and thereby outdo—beginning with Icarus—all those who had failed at it. Now he had to be dehypnotized by coming to feel the desire as the first conqueror of gravity to return to earth's lap!

There was just one confounded catch, alas the *conditio sine qua non:* he would have to have a great opponent who would whip up his ambition.

I set myself this difficult task, demanding special aptitudes and a readiness to make sacrifices. It meant practically becoming a *quasi* student of his for the period of instruction and his perfect *Doppelgänger* who pretended with devotion to imitate his development and the development of his thinking. Which meant becoming a replica of our man!

I needed a full third year before I mastered that. I confess that at the beginning I was many times tempted to desert the cause; once I had even bought myself an airplane ticket and was almost ready to remarry my former wife. What helped me at last were experience, determination, the Bible, and the thinking of one of my American colleagues, namely, Dr. Knight Dunlap (Knight Dunlap, *Personal Adjustment,*

McGraw-Hill Book Company, New York): "If a response habit is to be learned, or if a response pattern is to be made habitual, it is essential that the learner *shall have an idea* of the response that *is to be achieved* or *shall have an idea* of the change in the environment that the response will produce. . . . The important factor in learning, in short, is the thought of an objective to be attained, either as a specific behavior pattern or as the result of the behavior, together with a desire for the attainment of the object."

I have to tell you, it was a superb adventure, such as I have not enjoyed since, when we both swiped dogs in Pelhřimov and ate them fried under the pretense of having killed a bear. How much has this childhood talent helped me in my fantasy life!

I adapted myself to the fate of my patient to such a degree that I spent many a night crying about Kateřina Horová's lost love, yes, further: that I begged for money (!) to buy myself a small ticket-punch, shoulder-bag, and visored cap—but no: I don't want to bore you with details, anyway, what do you know of the small platform with its siding that reminds one of a toy train, or of the apartment in the resort section whose one window faced another window opposite only an arm's length away, what do you know of the unending nine years when I spoke nothing but the most basic words, when I restricted myself both with my mother and teachers to minimal communication and despite maternal tears and slaps ate no more than my body absolutely required for mere physical survival—all this is known today only to my doctor Miloš Makovec-Smith&Wesson. . . .

Forgive me! I should really strike out the above paragraph, or, better, rewrite the letter, but perhaps this passage will give you the best idea of how far my identification with our man has developed. Is there a better proof than that I—I!— have lost all interest in sex? Only so could I gain his full confidence and bit by bit and very naturally follow his entire process of the creation and realization of his phantasmagoric idea.

Truth to say, my temperament is not his, and therefore at the crucial point I could not take his path, the steepness and speed of which reflect his genius. Luckily Maxwell Maltz came to my rescue once again in the section entitled "How to Use Mental Pictures to Relax" (*Psycho-Cybernetics,* p. 56), where he advises anyone who for reason of age or weight can do neither yoga nor Czech calisthenics how to achieve the desired concentration. Beginning with the first sentence —"Seat yourself comfortably in an easy chair or lie down on your back . . ."—he reveals that he is counting on the intelligence of the atomic age.

Permit me to jump in this brief report over the weeks of most strenuous concentration during which he was my only staff and support with his quiet but sympathetic and, in the truest sense of the word, hypnotic presence. I want to get to the most essential: namely, to announce to you that my three-and-a-half-year effort was crowned by a result this morning of which neither I nor you nor your bosses dared dream three and a half years ago and that far exceeds your original assignment in every respect.

Now then: this morning, January 15, 19--, at 9:13.02 I completed my *first three steps* up the wall and after remaining a full thirty seconds in a horizontal position stepped back down to the floor *without wavering!*

I can therefore assure you in good conscience that no later than the fifth anniversary of the historic achievement of our man I shall be the second human being in the world who can duplicate his deed, at the same time the *first* who did so *on request.*

Greetings from your happy
Miloš Makovec-Smith&Wesson

[Note: Miloš Makovec-Smith&Wesson did not fulfil his promise as he was soon after arrested and convicted on a morals charge committed at an earlier date. In prison he showed signs of mental imbalance and he was therefore assigned to the psychiatric sanatorium in the former cloister of Na Brodě where he was subjected to the rule of Medical Director Dr. Polonyi (for this purpose rehabilitated), to whom he soon succumbed. The career of his devoted fellow student, friend, and Deputy Minister of Public Health, Dr. Stanislav Kapr, reached a somewhat better end. In the misguided attempt to avoid disgrace and to prove to the government that the costly project was crowned by success, he had the patient conducted to his garage shortly before the arrival of the commission. Taking Formalyn from the earlier mentioned story of Pyecraft as his model, he cut from the body of his own car heavy metal plates which he sewed into AJ's clothing so they would pull him down. The swindle was of course promptly discovered and Dr. Kapr's monthly salary was docked by 100 crowns. He was saved a heavier penalty and a public scandal only by the fortunate circumstance that at the time the scalpel of social criticism happened to be directed at the writers who once again had provocatively demanded the freedom of speech brusquely denied by the people.]

THIRTY-THIRD SESSION

held on December 24, 19--, in the private consulting room
[Prague 2, Karlovo nám., in the so-called Faust House] of
Dr. Sigmund Angst

*(in the transcript of the tape recording indicated by SA)
between him and patient AJ.*

[Note: Dr. Sigmund Angst, alias Adolf Angst, born in the
year 1900 in Prague, friend and intimate of Franz Werfel,
Franz Kafka, Max Brod, Egon Erwin Kisch, Valter Taub,
among many others, became a student and later close col-
laborator of the immortal father of psychoanalysis, Sigmund
Freud. As his assistant between the two world wars he was
periodically active in Argentina,* Bubeneč, Chile,* Dejvice,
England,* na Flóře, in Greenland,* Holland,* Ireland,*
Japan,* Karlín, Lapland,* Mozambique,* Nusle, Austria,*
Podolí, Rumania,* Smíchov, Turkey,* Úvaly, United States
of America,* Weinberg, and Cyprus.* That is why it comes
as no surprise that his way of expressing himself, reproduced
below, betrays now and then in its finer nuances a man who,
it has been aptly said, lives between two languages. In his
agitation over the loss of his great teacher, whom he had
served until the latter's death in London in 1939, he mistak-
enly flew to his home country without realizing that it had
in the meantime been occupied. He was supposed to have
been saved by an employee at the Prague airport of Ruzyně
who hid him in the basement of his small house, cared for
him and provided him with food and with news about the
war. The interesting thing is that Dr. Angst was not aware
he was in the hands of a quiet but persistent maniac: as late
as twenty years after the war he brought him to his basement

*With the exception of names marked by an asterisk (*) all are sections and suburbs
of Prague.

depressing news of a German-Russian invasion of the West Coast of the U.S.A. Dr. Angst was said to have been saved by a pure accident: owing to a badly designed tunnelling job on the Prague subway, underground workers broke into his hideout; they were very surprised when they were embraced by a crying old man who saw in them the supposed liberators of a foreign army unit. In recognition of his services he was presented with a private practice for experimental purposes. Requested to take on the case of AJ, he agreed, although he knew that he would be saddled with a task of unusually high demands on his psychic resources. He made it his lifelong custom, as an orthodox student of the master, to sit behind the head of patients so that they would not be able to read from the psychoanalyst's face how he reacted to their free-associations. At that time AJ understandably did not like to remain on the floor and spent most of his time on the ceiling. Dr. Sigmund Angst therefore conducted all sessions from a stepladder which at his age was an achievement commanding respect. The famous Sigmund Freud was born on May 6, 1856, in Příbor, Moravia; his teachings thus carry clear traces of Moravian folklore.]

SA: Young man, your birthday today, know that?
AJ: No.
SA: You're forty. Félicitations. A nice age, a whole life ahead of you.
AJ: Such a life isn't worth a damn.
SA: Whoa, don't despair, señor. Last session we got to—how they say?—where the bone is buried. What say we chop it up in honor of your birthday?
AJ: Makes no difference to me.
SA: A teensy weensy step we still need. I've been practicing fifty years. I'm the only one—top secret, bien sûr—allowed to analyze my great Master Sigmund. Was tickled so pink he let me take his—how you call it?—first name. I was the only student what best got the idea of

his favorite quotation from Faust: "Now is the air so filled by ghost/that to avoid him no one knows." Nu tak, kiddo, associate, free-associate already!

AJ: I don't feel like it.

SA: Meaning? Of course you feel like it. In our thirty-second session we came back to you—Jesus Christ, how you say?—dat's it: infancy. You remembered that you was nursed by bottle because your Mama no had milk. You said this was your oldest—no:earliest—memory. Right?

AJ: Yes.

SA: The bottle. What she look like?

AJ: A regular bottle.

SA: Watch it! Regular bottle can be any bottle. What this bottle remind you?

AJ: Nothing.

SA: C'est impossible, young man. Since Sigmund Freud everything reminds of everything. Free-associate already!

AJ: I don't know.

SA: Meaning? You don't know or you don't wanna? Peut-être reminds you of something dirty? Right?

AJ: It reminds me of nothing.

SA: Free-associate I'm telling you! Who gave you to drink from the bottle?

AJ: The neighbor.

SA: Comment? There you are. Absolyootely first-rate. So the bottle for you was a piece of the neighbor. Right?

AJ: I don't know.

SA: Well, like this we don't get nowhere. Il faut que vous cooperate. Free-associate, si? Your birthday today, furthermore—how you call it?—Holy Night today. You say this bottle is your oldest—no:earliest—memory, but when someone born on Holy Night, something he notices? No? Right?

AJ: I don't know.

SA: Don't you make me angry, you! You come into the

AJ: world and you make open your eyes, and—? Nu?
AJ: Someone cried.
SA: Vidyete? No, prosim! And then you saw Ker—Ker—
AJ: Chandelier.
SA: No! No!
AJ: Chandelier.
SA: Nebbich. You must of saw something else. How you call Kerzen in . . . right: candles.
AJ: I saw our chandelier.
SA: He's messing up toute ma conception. What you saw more?
AJ: Nothing more.
SA: Rien? Rien de tout? You didn't saw the—the candles? Because the candles and the bottles, they fit together, sabe? Know what I mean? Dat's a schrecklich sexual memory.
AJ: I saw the chandelier.
SA: Jesus Christ, he don't let me rest. Leastwise you know what it looked like?
AJ: Like always. Two cups and on top two globes.
SA: Whaaaat? Two globes? And there you say you didn't saw nothing.
AJ: I didn't see the globes because the cups were underneath.
SA: Un moment! Attention! But you wanted to see them? Yes or no?
AJ: For heaven's sake, leave me in peace with this. Maybe so, but the two cups were in the way.
SA: Boychik, we've got it. Dat's the model case what Mr. Freud was writing about. I can quote you by heart from Master Freud his fundamental work, *The Psychopathology of Everyday Life,* Chapter Roman Four, "On Childhood and Screen Memories": "A man of twenty-four has saved the following scene from his fifth year. He is sitting on a little chair in the garden of a summer house next to his aunt who is trying to teach him the

alphabet. This distinction between m and n gives him difficulties, and he begs his aunt to show him again how to tell one from the other. The aunt points out that m has a whole piece, a third stroke, more than n. There was no reason to question this childhood memory; it acquired its significance only later when it seemed suitable to take the symbolic place of another interest of the boy. Just as he formerly wanted to know what difference there was between m and n, he later tried to discover the difference *between boys and girls* and would certainly have been pleased to have the *same aunt as his instructress*. Then he discovered that the difference was a similar one, that a boy had *a whole piece more* than a girl, and at the time of this realization he recalled the respective childhood curiosity." Capito?

AJ: No.

SA: Meaning what, no? You no understand me? How, no? Crystal-clear, everything.

AJ: Not to me.

SA: O.K., then we'll get it. Now: Auntie tells this boy the letter m has one stroke more than letter n, and so he got it, when he noticed a boy has one more stroke than girl. Got it now?

AJ: No.

SA: He had for this aunt—no, how I say it?—he was sorry that his aunt didn't tell him. Kurzum, he loved the aunt. Ditto for your chandelier. Get it at last?

AJ: No.

SA: Herrgottimhimmel, what a schlemiel! You just loved your mother.

AJ: So?

SA: Only you no loved her as a mother, you loved her as a woman. Get it?

AJ: No.

SA: From birth you got fixated on two things, c'est à dire, three: your mother's scream and the two globes covered by cups. The cups are nothing else, señor, as—as a bosom. You know what bosom is?

AJ: No.

SA: Merde! Breasts! Listen: you wanted to see the breasts of your Mama, with what she wasn't able to nurse, so the breasts was covered, and dat's why you wanted to walk on the ceiling so you could saw the breasts from above at least, so I can tell you, boychik, all your flying around ain't nuthin but *displaced incest,* thank God, now we know, only one thing to do, go and sleep with your mother, then you're cured—zingo!

RECONSTRUCTION 12

(According to contemporary records)

When the 36
5 days had passed, which he had spent in solitary in the padded cell because he had pushed the aged Doc
tor Sigmund Angst without cause and without warning from his stepladder and with the brutality of a born sadist ground to dust the glasses of the man lying prone, so that at the conclusion of the project he could more easily do vi
olence to him, while the victim did not cease urging him to free-associate as to why he had done what he had done— it was then that the new Minister of Public Health ordered a continuation of the treatment, provided there was no repeated attack. It must be admitted that the drive behind this humane decision was not actually the Hip
pocratic Oath, but rather the pressure by leading representatives of rival psychological theories, who each wished to demonstrate the preeminence of his respective theory by means of AJ's case, it resembled a contest for a treasured

trophy, promising after the successive elimination of bio-psychiatry, psycho-cybernetics, and psychoanalysis a dramatic fin

ale, the next applicant was Head Resident Novosad from the psychiatric mammoth establishment in Zlolany where some three thousand psychopaths and neurotics were in treatment, mostly without hope, because right behind the wall of the block of buildings began the run

way of a military airport, supersonic planes with their sonic booms day and night created an atmosphere in which even perfectly normal inmates went mad, not saying what happened to the in

sane, Head Resident Novosad nevertheless achieved some not unnoteworthy results, some patients recovered if only to escape the earsplitting hell and to be allowed to return to their quiet boilermaking factories and riveting machines, besides he was six foot three and weighed 26

o pounds so that he was ca

pable of killing an ox with his bare fist, it was primarily this capacity that determined his choice, because despite the doctors' efforts Adam Juráček had altered incredibly in the six years since his trial, he had become bulky, swollen, and coarse, he let himself go and began to use crude expressions, his face lost its hu

man lines, the mean, cunning eyes embedded in fat between sparse bristles, recalled the physiognomy of a wild

boar, the Head Resident in the first few days circled around him in proprietary joy as though he had personally driven him home from the cattle market, Novosad was known as the most militant of all disciples of LSD, he was its prop and its sledge hammer, its anchor man, and its under

ling, in this case he rejected a psycholytic treatment which demanded a great number of small dosages of lysergic acid, choosing instead a psychedelic one which could be most aptly described as the eat-or-

die technique, day after day for almost three months he

prepared the valuable patient psychologically so that this famous drug which he was going to get but once, yet in a dosage never tried before, would be able to evoke in him unsuspected feelings and memories and catapult him back to the origins of his e

go from which he could make a second and more hopeful start, that, in short, a fantastic life experience awaited him which would thoroughly rattle his deformed personality, reverse the structure of all values, and fundamentally modify his every life attitude, his mistaken attitude towards gra

vity not excluded. The compound was scheduled to be administered on the first morning of spring, no one recalled that it was the anniversary of those events in K., when he had both conquered and been defeated, not even he remembered. The eu

phoria, which he had exposed to Dr. Polonyi and Assistant Professor Miloš Makovec-Smith&Wesson, had long since fled, he was not even disposed to get up to eat, whole days he sprawled apathetically on the ceiling where they had to attach a bracket for his bowl, otherwise he would have star

ved long ago. When they washed him on March 21, put clean pajamas on him, took him to the treatment room, and put before him a glass with a clear liquid, called in veneration the elix

ir of memory, he said to the Head Resident with a cynical grin:

"Hope I remember how my father made me . . ."

poured the 2000 gamma LSD down like a shot of whiskey and awaited the promised onslaught of feelings. They did not keep him waiting long. Ravel's "Bolero," chosen by Novosad as the opening piece of the musical accompaniment, and meant to accelerate the effects of the compound, suddenly lost its beat, yes, lost even the entire

score, the notes smashed into each other and wedged together like piled-up cars of a train, the first surge of the drug threw Adam Juráček instantly where normal patients rarely venture, and then only at the peak of the experience, he was lying in some kind of gelatinous paste with his knees resembling no knees touching his chin that was no chi

n, darkness all around him, but somewhere beyond the wall the hollow sound of a familiar voice, by what it said he recognized with amazement his mother, it took a good long while until he had o

riented himself, until he remembered when and where he had experienced it before, it was the emb

ryonic stage, he stretched himself luxuriously beneath the heart of his mother, who was just then in tears complaining to her newlywed husband, a train conductor, that her brother František was refusing to give her the cuck

oo-clock, which she loved beyond anything, the second wave grasped him even more violently, Juráček's gurgling baritone changed into a staccato soprano, he began to call the Head Resident, with whom he kept in verbal contact, father sir, and begged him to buy him a pennyworth of cookies, Novosad did not interrupt the dream so that at once the memory of his ge

nes began to unfold and, in the voice of the patient, whined his then six-year-old mother, who accompanied her father, a farmer, in the year of our Lord 1909 to the annual Xavírov fair, yet not even now did the chain of phantasmagoric memories tear, new waves of lysergic acid bombarded the genes like the alpha-particles the atomic nucleus, thereby liberating energy of still more deeply buried reminiscences so that at the end of the fourth hour the pithy old Czech of Juráček's great-great-great-great-grand

mother Květuše Rajda resounded, the same who offered the Wallenstein mercenary Hopner from Landshut the choice either to restore her honor by marrying her or to find his wretched end in a pig

sty, all this was kept secret from Novosad, so that the latter felt like Rabbi Lev who had put the slip with the magic Shem into the golem's mouth and now had to wait helplessly until it was revealed whether something good or something dead

ly had been created, nothing remained for him to do but attend the record player, he ascended the peaks of the classics as though he were hanging weights on the dumbbells of a weightlifter, he had reason to be more than satisfied with the reaction, the patient having done some breakneck pirouettes on the ceiling to Mozart, but when it came to Wagner he acted as though the latter had ripped his belly and filled it with rocks, they were myths and passions inherited from ancestors and their ancestors, their weight reduced him from a genius to a human wo

rm, until at last the "Missa Solemnis" flung him to the ground and the final vision he had was of God victoriously raising bo

xing gloves, and then he just lay like a cripple of Lourdes on the linoleum where his ordination took place, his nails digging into the cracks as though he wanted to burrow through to the planet's center of gravity, the weeping Head Resident summoned the entire staff to behold with their own eyes the peni

tent who refused to rise although the effect of the drug began to wear off, he was as weak as a child but most of all in love again with the fl

oor, in the evening he asked to be allowed to go into the garden so he could crush pieces of sod between his hands, they complied, Head Resident Novosad put on the final record "When the Saints Go Marching In" and personally supported the man so miraculously healed who would confirm the preeminence of LS

D, the detritus of seven unhappy years crumbled from Adam Juráček like dried mud, he devoured the earth with glances full of passionate feelings and put his feet down gently as though he were striding over the body of a beloved being, it was just that which was to prove fate

ful for him, the new feeling was not sufficiently fixed in

him, it had not yet solidified into certainty, when he wanted to leap over an unusually pretty mole hill which covered one of those mysterious routes into the interior of the earth, he pushed himself off a little more vigorously than would have been necessary, Novo

sad had not lied, the lysergic acid did indeed shake up the patient's personality, if his regrettable gift had so far had human dimension, now only the mind functioned, it was whipped up by the drug to the highest pitch with the intensity of a rocket engine and shot Adam Juráček ver

tically upwards like a hard-thrown ball, together with the Head Resident who supported him, his instinct for self-preservation changed Novosad's support to an embrace, he clung to his neck and ascended with him amidst wild screams before his terror subsided in a faint, luckily his patient took hold of him and, deluded by a belated LSD wave, remained hanging motionless in the air, about a mi

le above the countryside like a stationary satellite, at this point the radar screen at the Slolany airport picked up an ominous dot and the emergency squadron equipped with air-to-air rockets was skyborne. Thank God the two disturbers of the peace had only one metallic object between them, the Head Resident's stethos

cope, which was not enough to detonate the rockets, soon the reaction began to subside so that, having suffered no harm, they shortly made a soft landing on the terrain of the insane asylum, where Novosad instantly relinquished his function, while in the secret annals of world aviation another Unidentified Flying Object was recorded, the commanding officer of the airport was cited for brav

ery, and both pilots discharged from the service for asserting unendingly they had encountered a guardian

angel, although news of the fiasco reached only the very inner medical circles, duly censored at that—it was no more than "patient and Head Resident lost the ground under their feet"—it sufficed to put Professor Tajc, the head of the Institute for Research into Nervous Behavior, into the saddle, Ta

jc literally declared at a session of the Academy that a certain circus performance in a certain psychiatric institution had demonstrated the unscientific nature of certain therapeutic quackeries, in contrast to which the only genuine and promising approach to the treatment of advanced psychotics was made feasible by the behavioristic theory he repre

sented, he had figured correctly, before the month was over, he was in confidence summoned to the Minister and returned to the Institute with the craved trophy, he had his own study assigned to the patient, worked up with the aid of computers and the teachings of Pavlov and Volpe a long-range de

conditioning pattern, that

is, a gradual weaning of the patient from the ceiling and his gradual adaptation to the ground, the basic procedure became the prin

ciple of reward-and-punishment, Professor Tajc was in no hurry, he was going to make absolutely sure of his case, he devoted several months to a scrics of tests until he firmly established the fact that Adam Juráček's love was primarily directed to a small ticket-punch, a shoulder-bag, and a blue ser

vice cap with visor, Tajc's deconditioning program rested on the patient being permitted, as long as he stayed on the ground, to play

train with all the doctors and nurses, as soon as he forgot himself, however, and took his place on the ceiling, his favorite objects were taken from him for the following day, it was a brilliant idea even though it made considerable demands upon his entire staff, problems arose from the fact that his pupil kept broadening the game continually, for instance, he refused to have anything to do with a doctor or nurse who wouldn't show him a va

lid ticket, he didn't accept used ones and imposed fines on offenders which he remorselessly collected, they tried to fool him with the services of a deft graphic artist, but that attempt reached the district attorney's desk after three nurses were caught in the Prague-Bratislava express train with forged tickets, after that they stopped de

ceiving him, followed meekly his directions and strictly obeyed his transportation statutes, comforting themselves with the hope that this would more rapidly terminate his treatment, they did not

count on the likelihood that a man who had been locked up so many years by psychiatrists had necessarily changed his nature and was perhaps no longer yearning for life among nor

mal people. That is how it stood with him, he became used to it, made himself at home and because he was, apart from his defect, psychologically sound as a penny he realized that he could at no time and nowhere else expect more than he had now, he was in his own way happy although he did not obtain the hoped-for post of sta

tionmaster, as a train conductor, however, he spent a good deal of time among people and finally got more out of it, on several occasions he denied transportation to Professor Tajc himself when he came into the study during a trip or if he leaned out of the window, no won

der he was not in the least interested in his cure, and that is why, when they were beginning to be pleased that he had become a perfect earthling and was going to free them from their yoke, they discovered him again among the in

candescent lights, then they increased their punishment, but he was sufficiently adult to reconcile himself to a week's loss of his little ticket-punch, his shoulder-bag, and the vi-sored cap because he knew perfectly well he only had to mimic for a few days the good boy on the floor in order to have everything returned to him as a reward, while outside the Institute's walls he would have lost all con

cern for these items, that is how they tortured themselves

with him, they tottered in the vicious circle of his cunning and gambled away, slowly but surely, their reputations, while on the outside anniversaries passed, rain, snow, and hot spells, and governments replaced one another, the home country, Europe, and the world made for the threshhold of the third millenium, the scientific-technological revolution shattered idols, new generations fashioned new ones, and the distant events in the town of K. were buried by the avalanches of subsequent occurrences until there came that cru

el day when Professor Tajc retired and his staff scattered like a flock of chickens because the asylum was to be closed, nervous diseases had reached such proportions that a program was seriously considered to establish preventive institutions for those few individuals who had remained sane and whose presence created chaos among the rest, instead they were sent into retirement or the

woods, by coincidence the buildings were taken over by the representatives of a special outfit entrusted with special missions among citizens, A

dam Juráček welcomed them from the ceiling with his tongue stuck out in order to draw their full attention as soon as possible, on top of everything he had become vain, he had no doubt that their scientific passion would be set afire as it had been in all predecessors whom he had twisted around his little finger, they watched him with cool interest which in itself should have warn

ed him, they indeed asked to be allowed to keep him, a rather complicated business, since they belonged to a quite different kind of sec

tion, when they learned of this objection they uttered a snorting laugh and proposed that his name should simply be replaced by a num

ber, they'd simply take him over as part of the inventory, the caretaker who had repeatedly been fined a hefty sum for lighting a cigar in rooms that had been declared non-smokers' compartments, vindictively agreed, so that on November 8, 19--, by pure chance the anniversary of the Battle of Bílá Hora, Adam J

uráček ceased to exist and there appeared on the inventory the number 141041, specifying "1 pc. person without gravi

ty," a group of tall blue-eyed blond men took him over, they even wore the same ties and the same smiles, they looked like a national basketball team, his first impression of them was fa

vorable, without ado they let him accompany Professor Tajc to the steps of the train, or rather to the gate of the Institute, where he okayed for the last time a stopover and sa

luted him until the broken Tajc had disappeared beyond the turn in the drive, at that point the smiles faded from their faces like spring snow and they drily asked him the favor to desist from play-acting and accommodated himself to leading the regular li

fe of a working citizen, he recovered from his surprise and tried to escape from them to the ceiling, but they were quick

er, they jumped high like center court players made of rubber, caught him, pulled him back, and gave him the first sla

p in his life, and he had to watch how they smashed his little ticket-punch, ripped his shoulder-bag, and trampled on his ser

vice cap, whereupon an uncertain period elapsed which lasted possibly weeks or months but seemed to him a single unending ni

ght, which he spent alternately in a windowless room whose walls and ceiling were studded with long thin needles and in something like a strange dentist's chair upon which he half sat and half reclined, almost blinded under intense lights from which voices emerged, unlike human voices, and fired barrages of questions at him concerning gravitation in general and his relation to it in particular, even his numbed mind grasped that here Professor Tajc's principle of reward-and-punishment was being applied, however in a new and viler shape, the punishments were electric shocks, the reward the mere permission to retire, but even then he was not afforded any comforting alleviation, he had to relieve himself in the center of a large room which rather resembled a photo studio and behind the floodlights he saw the burning ends of cigarettes and heard indeed the click of shutters, he returned to his chair in greater tension than he was in before because it abandoned him to listening for more hours to the voices that alternately read him Newton's *Principia,* his mother's declaration that she was disassociating herself from him and demanded his deserved punishment, and a colorful description of Kateřina Horová's sex life, following that, they used to conduct him to his cell where he could rest for a while, never on the floor however, so that sleeping was practically made impossible for him, for the needles wounded him painfully, and he was able to float between floor and ceiling only when awake, he soon lost weight and strength and fell more and more often to the floor like a lump, then he was instantly picked up and lugged back to the chair where he heard the voices that accused him of scorning science, fatherland, humanity, nature, and anything that was firmly rooted in the ground, for a time he defied them in everything, he kept seeing the ruined little ticket-punch, the shoulder-bag, and the visored cap, hatred prolonged his resistance, but the utter isolation, the lack of any perspective, and their absolute psychological superiority gained more and more the upper hand, more and more he replied with a yes or a no, so that he escaped the electric charges, compared to which the shocks of Medical Director Polonyi looked like friendly tickling, until he was left with a last-ditch defense, and it was this defense that he decided to hold at any cost, like "We Are From Kronstadt," the only and yet the best film he had ever seen, whatever they did to him, he would not admit for anything in the world the correctness and incontestable validity of Newton's gravitational constants $F = k\frac{m_1 \times m_2}{r^2}$, where F is the force which two masses at the distance r exert on each other, perhaps that was due to the memory of a former colleague, the physics professor at the Pedagogical Institute in K., Vilibald Bláha, who was the only one never to have repudiated him, regardless of the fact that he hated him, a truth recognized, even though a terrifying one, had simply meant more to him than personal advantage, this they did not know though they knew everything else, indeed more than everything, and they were, let it be said in fairness, already exhausted and almost as emaciated as he, when they went home to rest after their shifts, they quarrelled with their wives and shouted for no reason at all at their children, to whom of course they were not allowed to mention their true activities, for officially they were concerned with research into the effect of atmospheric conditions on the quality of ergot, they had all the more reason to keep quiet as no one had entrusted them with case No. 141041, they were basically theoreticians, at that in a field from which society in its incomprehensible development had more and more removed itself, but they trusted their star, and when heaven itself had sent them this excellent opportunity of perfecting their theory, they had taken the bull by the horns, and now they were depressed that he had not yet been flattened, the game threatened to end in a stalemate, and a stalemate for them was like defeat, they stopped going home, they began to get collectively drunk, and feverishly tried to think of a move which would turn the encounter to their advantage until at last, at last they found it. When their exhausted but so far undefeated opponent asked next for the privilege to retire, not suspecting they had most cunningly rigged it themselves, he discovered in the ignominious photo studio, which he had come to terms with, something utterly incredible, namely, the toi

let bowl and its plumbing were attached to the ceiling,

behind the floodlights re-echoed drunken laughter, he heard bets being placed as to whether his ex

crement would overcome the gravitational pull and whether, if not, he would once again deny the teaching of the great Newton, sweat formed on his forehead, tears rose to his eyes, and he ca

ved in, without electric shocks, without even having been ordered to, he repeated in a broken voice the gravitational con

stants, without a word they left the job and went to sleep, they were not even capable of celebrating their triumph and were perhaps, possibly a little disappointed that something that would never happen again had come to an end, like true sportsmen who have defeated an opponent commanding respect, they let him sleep too, when he was first alone on the fl

oor after an indeterminate time, he pressed his cheek against it and kiss

ed it, yes, only now was it really a replay of the biblical return of the pro

digal, the work continued, but the atmosphere altered thoroughly, the electrical charges disappeared from the chair, the quartz-lights were turned off one after another, and from the dark appeared the blue-eyed, blond men who though did not return the little ticket-punch, the shoulder-bag, and certainly not the visored cap, yet he didn't even ask for them, the guilt feeling was as deeply embedded in him as the need to breathe, he was infinitely grateful when they offered him his first cigarette, he smoked it all in one long draught although he was a non-smoker, and he did two chapters of Newton's *Principia* on top of his regular assignment, he noticed how they fell apart, he felt new sympathy for them when he realized how much personally, how much sweat, they had sacrificed only because he had wrested himself from the natural order like a cancer cell, surely they had

had every right to simply carve him out of society's lap, to remove him surgically, but instead they offered him care of which no one nowhere would have dreamt, how he regretted he did not know their individual names, they all called each other Karel, but at least he learned to distinguish among them by the undertones in their hoarse voices, and when he had the good fortune to know the chief Karel to be personally in the room, he pursued him with puppy eyes, determined to do everything that might please him, he did not even notice that the needles had disappeared from the walls and ceiling, he used every spare second to lie on the floor of which he could simply never have enough, so that in due course the day had to come when all the Karels assembled with chrysanthemums in their lapels to close the case. The chief Karel asked him whether he was prepared to do everything, but really *everything* they might ask of him, he nodded so eagerly that he almost damaged his cervical vertebra,

"Very well," said the chief Karel suspiciously, "we'll test you, if you really want to please us, go and take a nice little walk on the ceiling . . ."

God knows he had never had a greater wish to comply with anyone, Kateřina Horová not excluded, than he did with his benefactor, without hesitation he turned his glance humbly to the ceiling but hardly had he caught sight of the smirking white surface than his whole body began to tremble as though he had received another electric charge and he began to ch

oke, he ducked instinctively and braced himself against more punishment, instead there came the sound of thunderous ap

plause, and his astonished eyes witnessed his beloved Karels congratulating one another and slapping him too on his thin shoulders, then it became clear to him that they weren't angry with him, on the contrary, they were praising him, even more, they had accepted him as one of their own, touched he responded to their flatteries and knew for certain that this time it was not a passing impotence that could leave him in the lurch at any time, but a *new quality,* that he had been granted the good fortune for the second time in his life to live through another such epoch-making day as that confounded March 4, 19--, had been for him, when full of pride he had been unfaithful to Mother Earth, whereas today he de

finitely had returned to her arms,

"I beg you," he turned with urgency to the chief Karel, "I beg you, Mr. Karel, tell me, confide in me, a person who I don't know for how many years was treated unsuccessfully by the greatest minds, what technique is it actually, good Lord, Mr. Karel, that is surely something for the Nobel prize in medicine . . ."

then he saw regret stealing to their faces as the chief Karel sadly replied that it was, alas, not an entirely new technique, maybe—well, certainly—more thoroughly exploited than in the past, at any rate a technique which did not fall into the domain of medical science and besides suffered from an ever-diminishing popularity among ever larger classes of people, so that in his case it had been applied more or less illegally, or, one might say, experimentally and only upon his express request, which they would now, at the conclusion of it, like him to acknowledge on this printed form, at

last here was something by which he could concretely show his gratitude, he enthusiastically reached for one of the pens which every one of the Karels proffered him headlong full of relief, and setting down with a flourish his name 141

041 in his best writing, inquired, in order to treasure it like a souvenir, what this technique was actually called, whereupon the chief Karel answered him with a foreign word, true enough, but it sounded to him like a folksong,

"brainwashing."

REPLY TO THE AUTHOR

by Mr. Alfréd Holeček, retired headwaiter, May 1, 2013.

Dear Sir:

To your appeal if any of your readers could kindly furnish information about Adam Juráček, I reply, namely, as follows: I was for a long time nephew to my Uncle Albín Holeček who was at the time in question a pensioner on the one hand, and, on the other, an immediate neighbor of the family of Juráček's father, a train conductor. From numerous talks with my Uncle, whose only and favorite nephew I was, I must take it at face value that Adam Juráček's inspiration would never have inspired him if Uncle Albín, the pensioner and neighbor, had not been the one to provide all the right conditions and incentives. But this influence was not accidental as you assume in your "Reconstructions," which I follow eagerly from instalment to instalment, but the very reverse. Time has come for me to make it known that my beloved Uncle, the pensioner, confided to me when I was still a little boy and brought him birdseed from Prague how he had fallen for his neighbor, Josefa Juráčková, then still the married wife of her husband the train conductor. It can therefore be assumed by rights that the short periods Adam Juráček spent looking after the parrot (and not a canary, as you write, he talks, he's been in my care ever since) were not as short as you describe, as my beloved Uncle, the pensioner, obviously did not go off on the errands you indicate, but quite opposite ones, so that the boy was purposely sent by his own mother to his apartment. Indeed I dare go further, namely, as follows: by studying the work schedules of train crews in K. for the year in which Adam Juráček was born—and I have access to these records as family relation of a railroad man—I have established that in the crucial March days Juráček's father was exclusively on night-shifts, from which a devastating conclusion emerges, namely, the following: Adam Juráček was not begotten by his father, the train conductor, but by my Uncle, the neighbor and pensioner. This my assertion I base on another certainty, namely, the following: exploiting the fact that my father, the headwaiter, was on night-shift too and that as a retired railroad man my Uncle had an unlimited railroad pass, which made it easy and cheap to travel daily to Prague and back, my beloved Uncle, the pensioner, begot me too, which later my beloved father, the headwaiter, confided to me personally, urging me in his drunkenness to call my Uncle Headuncle. Dear Sir, if you put these bits together as a writer, you are faced with a new situation, namely, the following: if my Uncle, the pensioner, was not only a neighbor of Adam Juráček but, on the contrary, also a father, while to me he was, on the contrary, a father and no Uncle, then Adam Juráček is my brother and vice versa! That is why I turn to you, Sir, as a writer, and answer your appeal with the demand, namely, the following: I demand herewith that you put your former statements publicly on the right track and remit me a percentage of your proceeds, such as my beloved brother Adam Juráček would have received, namely, the proceeds from his invention as well as the proceeds from your "Reconstructions" in instalments.

With deep respect and high expectations,
Alfréd Holeček-Juráček

[Note: The hypothesis of Alfréd Holeček, one of the most interesting, could neither be proved nor disproved, since the Lower Station in K., where the records were kept, fell victim to flames the day AH sent off his letter. Moreover, the parrot who was to have been the chief witness tragically got into the wiring of an electric range. The sole piece of evidence remaining, though it rather proves the opposite, is a letter by Alfréd Holeček in the fall of the year in which AJ performed his feat. It pays to quote from his letter of application for the job of headwaiter in the Prague Hotel "Esplanade": "At the same time I should like to squelch the rumor that has been passed around concerning myself, namely, the following: that I should in any way be related to, by blood or marriage, or that I should be acquainted with, that Juráček Adam who is to blame for the fateful, tragic, and reprehensible events in K. I should like to make the point that I have met him only once and that is when my Uncle forced me to, when I was no more than four. Already then I hated him and showed it, namely as follows: when he tried to take from me a lollipop I bit him in the ear, which also my Comrade Uncle, a rightful pensioner and a rightful transportation and sports official, can confirm who subsequently ceased to have anything to do with any of the Juráčeks, and who is at the moment buried in the Lower Graveyard in K."]

RECONSTRUCTION 13

(According to contemporary records)

When
in the fir
st days of the thi
rd millenium there came into force the General Agreement on Improvement of Human Affairs, sanctioned by UNO on the basis of the 333-year-old work by J
ohn Amos Comenius, and when they liquidated jails, insane asylums, and barracks, they happened to come across an old m
an in a certain Prague neighborhood who could recall neither his name nor his birthplace, he merely repeated the number 141041 without being able to explain what it meant, while the employees of UNES
CO elicited only this much, that he was ordered years ago by some kind of Karel to meet him there, he sustained himself on mushrooms which he cultivated in an atomic bunker, when they found out that the man was relatively spry and revealed an unusual interest in the conditions of railway
stations, it was decided to dispatch him to Darlington in England, which had just been designated a home for retired European railwaymen in hon
or of the 175th anniversary of the trial journey of the world's first locomotive, "The Rocket," invented by George Stephenson, the run having taken place on September 21, 1825, on the Stockton-Darlington section at a speed of 19 kilometers per
hour (fully loaded), they summoned a helicopter by telephone and urged the man, while they were waiting, to go to a nearby café and have himself a glass of Pilsener which since January 1, 2000, was being distributed free, for the doctors had reliably proved that it was the most effective means of controlling pop

ulation growth, incidentally, without side-effects. The number person walked out into the street, succeeded in negotiating uncleared snow piles, and entered a roomy bar where a loud hubbub of voices greeted him, he stood bewildered at the door and stared at the emp

ty surface of the room, which looked as though it had just been painted, nowhere a table or chair, he looked in vain for the source of this very realistic background noise until it occurred to him to glance at the ceiling, the ceiling was chock

full of students from the nearby Faculty of General Physics who were still celebrating the jubilee, his first im

pulse was to cry out, something in him rose like sobbing, something told him excitedly that his place was by rights up there among the light

fixtures and among the boys, who reminded him so much of something, he even dug out of his memory the name Václav Kl

okoč, but in the next second a painful cramp took hold of his muscles as though lightning had struck him and he humbly lowered his gray head and whispered to himself what seemed like a magic spell:

"Capital F equals k times m one times m two divided by r to the second . . ."

and that was all there was to be reconstructed out of the
moving fate of the professor of Physical Education and
Drawing at the Pedagogical Institute in K.,
Adam Juráček, a Czech genius forgotten b
y the world, who in his own time under
the prevailing conditions was so far
ahead that he was neither heard,
looked at, nor given belief, so
that the failure of his deaf
and blind contemporaries en
ables us, his descendants,
to take part as mere ob
servers in the unending
struggle of universal
knowledge, wheth
er the first who
could stay on
the ceiling
without
the
aid
of mechanical devices was the black preacher from Missis-
sippi, Every Whitehouse, or the Peking activist Tung Fang
Chung, or the Komsomol member Ivan Fedelovich Bodrik,
most li
kely
of
a
l
l
.